This book is dedicated to organizations like Habitat for Humanity that are making it possible for low-income individuals and families to own their own homes.

It is also dedicated to the mother-daughter HGTV "Good Bones" team of Mina Starsiak Hawk and Karen E. Laine. They have recently completed their eighth and last season of this show. Although the Nailed It Home Reno series is not based on them or their work, their show, which has focused on bringing some of the older neighborhoods in Indianapolis, Indiana, back to life, was the inspiration for this cozy series.

This book is also dedicated to woodworkers like my late father, Richard Youngman, and my husband, Veryl, who have employed and continue to employ their unique skills with wood.

WRENCHED AT THE REINDEER RUN

A FLORIDA HOLIDAY MURDER MYSTERY

BOOK 7

BARBARA BARRETT

Paperback ISBN: 978-1-948532-65-5

CHAPTER 1

"Can't help you," said Terry Seiser, owner of Seiser Lumber and Hardware. I hadn't even introduced myself, let alone begun my spiel about donating to the Reindeer Run charity event, and he was already saying no.

Surely he'd misunderstood. "I'm Rowena Summerfield, co-owner of Nailed It Home Renos. Perhaps you didn't hear me say I'm asking for your help with this charity event to support low-income housing here in Shasta."

That's Shasta, Florida, a small city in central Florida. I'm a former homicide detective who took a disability retirement after a horrible on-the-job vehicle accident kept me from field work. After several months of rehab, self-hating, then self-discovery, I became an interior designer and opened Nailed It with my daughter, Valerie. These days, I sometimes consult with my former employer on homicide cases.

"I heard, but I'm not interested," he said dismissively. Where was his holiday spirit? Christmas was only two weeks off.

I couldn't believe his attitude. I should've let it go and left, but something made me try one more time. "I'm not asking for much. Just some rope and clips to make a crowd divider."

Seiser wasn't a tall man, but he had a barrel chest, which I hadn't noticed until he stood up from where he'd been bent over sorting screws of various sizes. He pulled himself up to all of his approximately five-foot-six splendor and, for the first time since I'd entered the store, gazed directly at me. His head shape matched the rest of his body, round except on top, where it was flat, and his eyes, tiny and set apart, blazed like an angry boar's. "I said I'm not interested. Do us both a favor and leave."

I held up my hands in faux surrender. "Fine, I'm leaving, but only after you tell me what's going on here. I barely set foot in this place and you were already against me. What have I ever done to you?"

His head came forward and his eyes narrowed, making his face look even more piglike. "I can't believe you have to ask. You don't even remember the last time we clashed."

"Uh, we clashed?" He had me there. I had no recollection of mixing it up with the man. I'd only dealt with him once that I recalled. That was in the early days of Nailed It.

"Shoulda known. I don't even rate a small embarrassed memory in your book. You accused me of taking advantage of a woman in a new business. Just because the manufacturer chose to up their prices after I gave you a quote based on their status quo. You chewed me out royally, said you'd tell all your friends to avoid doing business with me."

I started to rebut his statement, then cut myself off. Now that he'd mentioned overcharging me based on an earlier estimate, I vaguely remembered something like that happening a few years back. At least three. I was so new in the home rehab business, and a woman in a man's world to boot, I must've pushed that whole incident to the back of my mind. Not remembering was so unlike my cop persona, where my mind was like a computer when it came to human behavior.

Even though I wasn't particularly proud of those actions, there was no need for him to hold a grudge this long, although the more I was in the construction business, the more I realized hard feelings sometimes did carry through the years. I'd become much more circumspect in my dealings with subs and service providers as a result. No point in making matters worse with this particular merchant. I didn't think his attitude was completely aimed at me this morning, but I wouldn't push him further. "I'm sorry you feel that way." I left my card on the counter well out of his reach. "If you change your mind in the next day, let me know."

I didn't exactly run out of the building, but I didn't linger either.

I drove away immediately but stopped a few blocks away at a drive-through coffee stand. I needed caffeine. Lots of caffeine, which I would imbibe as soon as my hands stopped shaking.

I took a quick gander at myself in the car's dropdown mirror. Still the same short dark brown bob and brown wideset eyes. I didn't look browbeaten by that last experience. I just felt that way.

The nerve of that guy! Okay, I admit to having the gall to challenge my bill once upon a time. Perhaps I could've delivered my ire in a lower volume, but he was the one at fault. He could've warned me prices were about to change.

Enough poor-me time. The only way to deal with this setback was to move forward and find something that did work. I had agreed to take on decorating the community center for the cocktail party the night before the Reindeer Run, a 5K marathon, when the person in charge suddenly left town to care for an ailing parent. She'd been so worried about her father, she hadn't done any planning as far as what they were calling the Reindeer Run Rendezvous was concerned.

I must've been out of my mind to say yes with only a week to put this together, but it was Shane Bolton, manager of my boyfriend Chuck Dawson's restaurant, who'd begged me to take pity on him and say yes. Through Chuck I'd learned this was Shane's first attempt to reach out to become more active in the community. I wanted to help him. Plus, due to interaction with the neighbors on our current project, Val and I had realized it was time Nailed It gave back to the community that was supporting us.

Decorating the inside of the community center where the event was to be held had seemed like a slam-dunk when Shane first asked. But then my interior designer brain engaged and started putting together a plan that called for not only more time than I had for construction but also supplies and materials neither I personally, my business or the event committee could afford. Thus, the need for donations. Soliciting this type of help was not in my wheelhouse. Exhibit A: what I'd just experienced with Seiser. Granted, he wasn't the most socially responsible person around, but would everyone else I planned to contact have similar complaints about me personally that would preclude them from contributing?

My phone rang as I was about to return to the duplex I shared with Val to list donor options on the white boards I kept there for homicide investigations.

"How's it going?" Chuck asked. The man had incredible radar where I was concerned. At times, he seemed to know what was on my mind before I did.

"Not so well. I had no idea my business dealings would come back to haunt me when I returned to ask for donations."

He didn't reply immediately. "Yeah, that can happen. You know what they say about burning bridges. Who said no?"

I related my brief encounter with Seiser.

"You picked the worst of the lot to start with. Wish you'd mentioned your plan to approach him to me before you descended upon him. I might've been able to prepare you."

"You know him?" Why would my guy who owned a deli, a restaurant and a wine bar have interacted with the owner of a hardware store and lumberyard?

"Not well. By choice. Ran into him a few times at chamber of commerce meetings. Not a happy camper. Views the world with scorn." Another pause. "I'm sorry you had to tangle with him first thing."

"I'm glad you called when you did. I was feeling sorry for myself. At first I blamed myself for approaching him the wrong way, but the more I've thought about it, I don't think there was anything I could have done to change his mind."

"Good decision."

"Now I'm rethinking not only my approach but the whole design plan. I was just about to head home and start listing options."

"Before you do, tell me what you're thinking," he said.

"First, I don't have much time to do anything. We're down to five days before the event. Therefore, my plan must be simple, meaning whatever I need to put it together, I must obtain posthaste."

"If you don't mind sharing, what were you planning to do at the community center?"

"I thought I'd set up something to look like the race course by roping off three corners of the room so it would look like those in attendance were there to root on the runners on the outside. Not a complicated look but very dependent on getting enough rope and stanchions, which don't have to be real, just posts of some type to tie the rope around."

"Intriguing idea."

"That's all you have to say about it?" I asked. What was he seeing that I wasn't?

"How much are you committed to it?"

"Earlier this morning, at least ninety-five percent. That number has gone down considerably now. But I must replace it with something else immediately."

"What you were going for would be a great tie-in to the race itself and would probably look pretty great," he said tentatively. "Until people started to arrive. If Shane has been drumming up as much interest in the marathon as I think, there will be a crowd. Your design will cut off ten to twenty percent of the available floor space. People like to be close for events like this but not on top of each other."

That was his kind way of telling me to scrap the whole idea. Was it possible Terry Seiser had done me a favor? Not intentionally, but that seemed to be how it was working out. "Okay, I get what you're saying. I suppose I could fall back on the old standard, Christmas trees. But I don't have a budget to buy even one. I could maybe foot the bill and take it home afterwards? I haven't had time to get one of my own yet."

"I have a Christmas tree here at The Sandpiper. It's already decorated."

"That's very generous, Chuck, but that would mean transporting a decorated tree from your place to the community center and back again afterwards."

A couple beats went by. "Not necessarily. What if Shane moved the party here? We're already contributing the hors d'oeuvres, appetizers and wine. And we're already decorated."

For one glorious moment I was ready to cave and thank him repeatedly. Then the reality of what he was offering hit. "Chuck! That is so generous, but it's too generous. You'd have to close the restaurant and the wine bar for one night and lose all that revenue. I can't ask you to do that."

"You didn't. I offered. When is this party supposed to take place? Surely it's not more than a couple hours? We could work around that time and either close early or open late."

"You make it sound so doable, but no, I can't ask you to do that. It would negatively affect your staff as well. They would be earning less, especially around the holidays."

"Don't worry. I'll take care of them."

Meaning he'd pay them their usual wages and supplement their tips out of his own pocket. As tempting as his offer was, I couldn't let him do that.

CHAPTER 2

n the end, I accepted his offer, on condition that Shane approved the change. Shane was absolutely delighted with the idea when the two of us went to him with it fifteen minutes later. "That is so good of you, boss," he told Chuck.

"Don't credit me too much," Chuck replied. "This is great advertising for the restaurant and wine bar for those who've never been here. And there are a few folks in town who haven't." He grinned.

That night, as we relaxed over a cozy dinner of turkey tetrazzini and kale salad, I continued to express my appreciation. "Thank you again for your generosity. Maybe you should consider the loan of The Sandpiper your Christmas gift to me."

"No way! I've already got something else in mind."

"You do? What?" I sounded like I must have when I was a kid trying to get my parents to spill their secrets ahead of time. With the Rendezvous decorating and finishing up Mehaffy House, our current rehab project, on my mind, I'd almost forgotten to think about Christmas gifts. I smiled to myself. Almost, but not entirely.

If men could emulate the Mona Lisa smile, that's what he gave me. "You know I can't do that. You'll just have to wait."

"Okay. But I owe you for donating The Sandpiper."

"I'll remember that," he said, his eyes twinkling. "The restaurant and wine bar are in good shape thanks to you, but one of these days, maybe we should consider updating the deli."

"Really? I've always liked its casual atmosphere."

"Just a thought. I'm sure we can find a way for you to repay me at some point." He had the audacity to wriggle his eyebrows. "So? What will you do with your spare time now that the decorating has essentially been done for you?"

"Not entirely. I'm meeting with Shane tomorrow morning to go over the layout for serving. We'll need to move some of the tables to allow for people standing around, and we'll need to figure out where to serve the appetizers and hors d'oeuvres, since we won't be doing table service."

He studied me, his forehead wrinkling. "Oh. Guess I thought it would go like a typical serving night. People seated at tables, my wait staff circulating throughout the room offering food and wine on trays."

"Is that a deal-breaker?" I asked.

"No. I'll leave the layout up to Shane, with your input, of course."

I took his hand in mine. "You are the greatest. You know that, don't you?"

"Anything I can do to please my lady." He was so sincere. He didn't sound corny at all. True, his gesture was for charity, but it was also a huge statement of his love for me. Love? I used that word again. It had come up a few times recently, but it was so precious, neither of us wanted to overuse it. Still, it was one more sign that things between us were getting progressively more serious. The time was coming when I'd have to decide what to do about it. I was a fifty-seven-year-old widow of thirteen years. Was it really necessary to make a legal commitment in this day and age?

The next few days flew by. Mehaffy House, an older, two-story-plus-attic house, was reaching the point where I needed to be present to direct the placement of all the furnishings. Thanks to Chuck's generosity, I'd found time to invest there, as soon as Shane and I could finalize plans for the Rendezvous.

"I couldn't believe my luck when you called to ask if I was okay moving the venue to The Sandpiper. This means I can spend more time here at work and still be planning this part of the event," Shane told me when we first met. "I still have to check in with the rest of the marathon committee from time to time, but this change frees me up considerably."

"Thank Chuck for suggesting the Rendezvous be held here. Truth be told, he took pity on me when my first day of attempting to solicit donations for the decorations tanked." I gave him an overview of my experience with Terry Seiser without mentioning the jerk's name.

"The guy at the hardware store who didn't want to hear you out? By any chance, was his name Terry Seiser?"

"Uh, yes. I was trying to take the high road by not naming him. Do you know him?"

The smile that had been present on Shane's face since we'd starting talking about the venue switch disappeared. His lips firmed up. "Yeah. Haven't seen or talked to him recently. By choice. But once upon a time, I worked in that same store. For his dad, Bill Seiser. Nice guy. Can't explain how his son grew up to be such a dirtbag, but he was already like that when the two of us worked for Bill. I'm sorry your paths crossed."

"Not your fault. Apparently I had words with him a few years ago when my bill came in much higher than he'd led me to expect. I'd forgotten the incident and moved on. He hadn't."

"Carries a grudge. He was already like that then. Sorry you had to deal with him on my account, but one good thing about it. His attitude resulted in this change."

Only now did another question occur to me. "What about

publicity for this late change of plans? Do you have to recall any flyers or public service announcements?"

"In this day of the internet, all it took was a few online modifications and we've been good to go."

"Terrific! One less thing to worry about."

"You should really be worried about the fact anyone can walk in here any time of day," said a male voice behind me. A grizzled, self-important male voice.

"Sorry, sir, we're not open yet," Shane said in his usual placate-the-customer voice.

"Daryl Henson doesn't tend to observe those rules," I told Shane. "Shane Bolton, manager of this restaurant, this is former vice cop Daryl Henson." I tried to keep my disdain out of my voice. Not an easy feat. Hercules "Herc" Morgan, my former homicide partner, and I had never been friends with the man when I was on the force, and the few recent encounters we'd had with him hadn't been very cordial either. We suspected the guy was dirty. Even ran across direct evidence in a recent murder case that indicated he'd taken bribes from a former madam to avoid her place, but it was too late to do anything about it.

"Daryl Henson? You're the guy who's handling security for the Reindeer Run," Shane said. "

"Security?" I said, my astonishment coming through in my tone.

"That's right," Henson replied. "Gotta do something to keep myself busy in my retirement. Don't have the wherewithal to paint houses."

"I do the interior design," I said, realizing too late he was baiting me, just like always.

Having succeeded in delivering his blow, Henson turned his attention to Shane. "Heard there'd been a last-minute switch in location for the party the night before the run. That your decision?"

"Yes, it was," Shane replied. "We ran into some snags decorating the community center, so my boss offered to open up his place, where most of the decorating is done."

"The move should've been run past me first," Henson said self-importantly. "This place could involve all kinds of security problems."

"This is a restaurant and wine bar, Mr. Henson. We face potential security problems from out-of-control patrons all the time, but I'm pleased to say we've had few incidents. Nothing serious."

"Nonetheless, Ellen Garvey, who's chairing this event, asked me to check things out."

"Right. I called Ellen to run the change of venue past her before we made it official. She was delighted and gave us her blessing. In fact, when I asked if I needed to inform anyone else, she said not to worry. She'd take care of those details. Apparently one of those involved informing you."

"Yeah, well, I told her exactly what I just told you. I shoulda been consulted first."

Shane invested a lot of his work time ensuring things ran smoothly at the restaurant. Much of that effort went into smoothing the ruffled feathers of irate customers. That persona went into action now. "No slight intended, Mr. Henson. May I call you Daryl, since we'll be working closely together the rest of this week? I'm Shane. Why don't I show you around the place now. I'll take note of any potential issues you point out." He switched his attention to me. "We're done for now, aren't we, Ro?"

Even if we still needed to talk, this was no time to mention it. "Right. I'll call if anything else occurs to me." I pivoted to leave, then turned back. "You're in very competent hands, Daryl."

I didn't give him a chance to answer but instead booked my way out of there as fast as I could. I called Herc once I was in the car. "You won't believe who's heading up security for this charity event I'm involved in."

"Hello to you, too," he answered. "I'm not in the mood for Twenty Questions. Who?"

Uh-oh. What was up with him? I hadn't heard through Val's

live-in boyfriend, Jim Watkins—Captain James Watkins, my some-times boss when I consulted for the department—that there'd been any murders lately. Maybe that was the problem. My friend was feeling bored.

I told him it was Henson. "Have you heard anything about him setting up his own security practice?"

"No, and something as juicy as that woulda been common knowledge around here within twenty-four hours of him setting out his shingle. Thought he said he'd retired? Didn't we learn he'd been taking money for years to look the other way with petty criminals?"

"Maybe he burned through it. He didn't sound particularly thrilled to be working again. He came down hard on Shane for not bringing him up to speed on the venue change when the event chair had already taken care of that."

"Probably the dogs. I remember how he was always broke because he'd put his money on the wrong contender."

"How'd you like to be my guest at the Reindeer Run Rendezvous? Chuck will be too involved making sure nothing goes wrong. I could use someone to help me fend off Henson."

"Ah, Ro. You know how much I hate those frou-frou things."

"What if you could invite Luann Cory to be your guest? No reason why I couldn't invite a couple. Wait, isn't she participating in the run?" Luann, assistant Shasta fire chief, was the first woman Herc had dated in a long time.

"Yeah." He groaned. "Things between us were just heating up after Thanksgiving and spending the night in the attic of your so-called haunted house, and then she got involved training for this race."

"She's probably already made plans to attend the Rendezvous the night before."

"What if she's asked someone else to go with her?" He sounded like a preteen afraid to talk to the girl of his dreams.

"You'll never know until you ask." Why did I have to keep

reassuring him as far as this woman was concerned? From what I observed at Thanksgiving, she was into him.

"Promise you won't keep running off to check on things if I have to come stag?"

"I don't anticipate anything going wrong. Shane Bolton and I have this in hand."

It was almost like I was tempting fate with that statement. Would I never learn?

THE ZIPPER ON MY COCKTAIL DRESS STUCK AS I WAS GETTING DRESSED for the Rendezvous on Friday night. That should've been a sign to take off the dress, crawl under the covers in my nightgown and skip the party.

"I suppose you think you could do better?" I told my tuxedo cat, Jason. He'd wandered into my bedroom a minute before. Nothing got by him when it came to anything going on in my home. Of course, he couldn't jump up and tackle the pesky zipper on his own. His contribution was to sit there on the bed and eye me, like his stare-down would fix things.

Good soldier that I was, I patiently fiddled with the thing for ten minutes until it gave way. Jason offered a knowing look, at least a knowing feline look, like that had saved the day. Maybe it had. His presence had helped me calm down and focus.

I was only a few minutes behind schedule when I walked into The Sandpiper an hour before the event was to start, my good mood restored.

"I'm so glad you're here," Shane called as he approached me. This was not the calm, in-control restaurant manager I left earlier in the day when we went over last-minute details for the evening. "The roof is caving in. Well, not literally. That might be easier to fix."

CHAPTER 3

drew him over to one of the tables we'd left in the room and made him take a seat. I dashed off to the service stand and was back in seconds with a glass of water. "Drink first, then we'll talk."

My commanding cop voice had momentarily taken over. He didn't object but took a few sips instead. "Thanks."

"Now then, tell me what's up."

"First, one of the microwaves in the kitchen chose tonight to act up. It can be fixed, but right now that would take too much time. Then I remembered the one in the wine bar, which Lorna uses on occasion to heat up appetizers." Lorna Varney managed The Piper, the wine bar adjacent to the restaurant.

"Okay. That must've been a frustrating few minutes," I said, not sure if that was the kind of thing he wanted to hear or not.

"That was just for starters. Then the florist you got to donate the poinsettias was late delivering them. I should've let you go get them earlier today when you volunteered to pick them up, but you've spent so much time on this event, I thought you needed a few hours off to relax. I just got through arranging the plants before you arrived."

I knew I should've pushed him more to let me do that much.

But what was done was done. I surveyed the area of the room where we were clustering the plants near the Christmas tree. "You did a great job setting them out, Shane."

"Thanks. But I'm used to dealing with setbacks like those two problems. Normally, I could've handled them and broken a sweat. It's that former cop who's crowned himself King of Security who's been getting to me."

Daryl Henson had struck again. "What's he been up to?" I really didn't want to deal with the man any more than I had to, and dealing with him really was Shane's responsibility, but he seemed so flummoxed, I thought I should volunteer.

"He wants to close off the back entrance, the one that goes directly into The Piper. We can't do that. There are fire laws. What kind of Security guy doesn't recognize the danger of allowing only one point of access to an event?"

"Did he say why?" If I planned to confront the man, I needed to know what I was dealing with.

"Something about not allowing participants to stroll in and out. Does he have no idea how these social events go? People know we've got that secret garden area out behind the wine bar. On a night like this, some folks may want to, uh, take advantage of it."

"I'll see if Chuck will tackle that one. Don't let Henson get to you. He hasn't been in charge of much of anything lately. Sounds like he's taking advantage of the title."

"That wasn't all," Shane continued. "He wants to limit the number of drinks anyone can have. In a way, I get his point. The less alcohol imbibed, the less chance of incidents. But this won't be an unruly crowd. These folks are here to support the marathon and the charity. No one will get out of hand."

"You're not leaving open bottles out on the bar or on the tables, are you?" I asked.

"No way! Despite the so-called gentility of the crowd, no one's perfect when the alcohol flows freely. We'll be serving drinks on trays. I told the servers after they finish circulating each time to hold off ten minutes."

"Good plan. Did you share it with Henson?"

"The guy kept cutting me off."

"Sorry, Shane. This one's yours. I know you're up to explaining to him in no uncertain terms that managing alcohol consumption is your job."

He blew out a breath and straightened his shoulders. "You're right, Ro. Guess I let my jitters about overseeing this event get to me. All I needed to hear was your voice of reason."

"Why don't you take a short break and catch your breath? Go back to Chuck's office and chill a bit."

He hugged me briefly and took off. I went in search of Chuck to alert my guy to Henson's access plan.

The first hour went well, as guests arrived and were treated to drinks and appetizers. My job as decorator done, I now helped Shane by greeting attendees as they entered the room. I'm not usually comfortable in this type of social situation, but this evening I felt a different vibe. Everyone seemed so up, probably because of the approaching holidays, but also because of the excitement mounting about the upcoming race. I didn't have to appease or placate anyone, just point them in the direction of the food and drinks.

Early on, Ellen Garvey made it a point to thank me for my part in the evening's festivities. She struck me as being in her mid-forties, about a decade younger than me, but crow's feet were already starting to appear around her deep green eyes. They were nicely set off by the emerald green satin suit she wore. I'd met her at one or two other social events over the last several months, but no close friendship had grown out of those encounters. We were both busy women whose careers were taking us different directions. She was a suddenly wealthy widow, and I rehabbed older houses.

"I was so pleased to hear about the change in tonight's venue, Mrs. Summerfield. Holding the event here at The Sandpiper was a dream on my list. I never thought it would become an actuality. I plan to thank Mr. Dawson, but I haven't seen him yet," she said.

"Call me Ro, please. And he's Chuck. He's probably keeping the kitchen staff company so Shane can be in charge out here. Shane has worked hard to make this evening come together."

"And I'm Ellen. I couldn't agree more about how well things have gone with Shane handling this evening's activities. All I must do is say a few words to greet everyone and then my part for tonight is over."

She'd just left me to find the microphone when I heard shouting near the wine bar entrance.

"Let go of me, Bolton. I have just as much right to be here tonight as you," a male voice shouted.

Terry Seiser had deigned to come to the party? He was attempting to get past Shane to enter the restaurant.

"You wouldn't help us with decorations. How does that get you an invite?" Shane said in a voice I'd never heard him use before, even with unruly customers. His complexion had gone as red as the poinsettias decorating the room.

"I support this charity," Seiser returned, his voice steely. "I just don't support you, Bolton. I'd already told Ellen I'd be happy to help, but when I read you were in charge of whatever this is tonight, I switched my support to constructing the viewing stand at the end of the race tomorrow."

"You're doing that?" Shane asked. "What's in it for you?"

"Same thing you're getting from your little show tonight. Stepping up to help the community."

"Since when have you cared one fig about the community? All you care about is making money."

I recalled how Shane had called Seiser a dirtbag who carried grudges. Only from what I was hearing now, Shane, unfortunately, seemed to be the one bringing up grudges. Other than refusing to back off, Seiser was maintaining his cool.

Shane grabbed Seiser by the upper arms in an attempt to push him back out the door, but the intruder held his ground. Shane removed his right hand from the other man's arm in order to deliver a blow, but his fist was deflected by none other than Daryl Henson.

"Let's take this outside, boys," Henson said in an official law enforcement voice.

Herc appeared from out of nowhere to help his former nemesis break up the fight. Could this scene get any more surreal?

Ellen Garvey, who'd changed course from the microphone at the front of the room to head back to the disturbance, changed course again and grabbed the mic. "Sorry, folks. Just pre-race jitters. Nothing to be concerned about. Please go back to your conversations and drinks."

My six-foot-plus ex-football player hunk and love of my life, Chuck, appeared at my side. My guy looked particularly handsome tonight in his new dark gray suit, which went particularly well with his short salt-and-pepper buzz cut. "Was that Shane I saw being led outside?"

"Uh, yes. The other guy was Terry Seiser, the one who turned me down for decorations earlier in the week. At the time, he made it sound like he wouldn't do it because of me, which probably was part of his reason. But he also resented Shane from way back. He seemed to know exactly what button to push tonight to make himself appear to be the injured party."

"I'd better go check on things outside," Chuck said. "Can you take over for Shane until I return? Something tells me my trusty manager will need to go off and lick his wounds the rest of the evening."

"Yes, of course. Go. I'll help Ellen Garvey reassure our guests nothing is amiss." Although I wasn't sure that was the case.

Chuck returned along with Herc after a few minutes. "I sent

Shane home to cool off," Chuck told me. "Henson said he'd remain with Seiser until Shane was out of here."

"Can't believe I was actually helping Henson," Herc said. "But I'm glad you warned me ahead of time he'd be here. For once, I don't have anything negative to say about him. He was johnny-on-the-spot to keep that argument from getting out of hand, although it appeared to be mainly a matter of calming down your friend. The other guy reminded me of a snake charmer. All he had to do was keep playing his tune and your friend got more and more agitated."

"Funny, that. Shane never loses his cool. He told me he knew the guy way back. There must be extreme feelings there."

To my surprise, Ellen Garvey also fancied herself a bit of a stand-up comedian. Her jokes went a long way toward regaining the earlier tone of the evening. "A funny thing happened on my way to this mic," she'd begun. She attempted to convince the crowd they'd just witnessed a skit featuring two of the event's volunteers, only they'd neglected to inform their crack security guy, who thought it was real and broke it up before they could finish.

I wondered how Henson would've reacted to being blamed for the abrupt end of the so-called drama. At least she referred to him as a "crack security guy."

The race was to begin at seven in the morning. Short night, but I felt I should show up at least for part of it to show my support. Chuck would've gone with me, but he wanted to check the restaurant and wine bar to make sure the cleaning crew had put everything back in order, and after that, he planned to stop by Shane's.

The run was to take place in Busse Park, a large plot of land donated to the City several years ago by an entrepreneur who'd made his fortune in early internet marketing and leveraged it into a monumental online magazine empire before selling it a few years ago and retiring to Fiji. He'd run high school races in the park as a boy and purportedly didn't want to see it sold off to developers once he left town. I didn't come here often, but it was a great place to sneak off to when I needed to think by myself.

I barely got inside the front entrance when I was stopped by a patrol car. "Sorry, ma'am. You can't go any farther." She was a younger officer who didn't recognize me.

"I came to watch the race. Isn't there any visitor parking?"

"The race has been canceled," she said tersely. "At least for today."

"Canceled? What happened?"

She bit a lip, wanting to say more but held back by orders.

"It's okay to tell me. I'm Rowena Summerfield, formerly Lieutenant Summerfield. I was a homicide detective for the city."

"Oh, Lieutenant Summerfield. I've heard about you. You still work with the force from time to time, right?"

I nodded.

"Are you here for the accident?"

I wanted to act like I was, but I didn't want to get this young woman in trouble. She seemed new and a bit overwhelmed by the situation. "Accident? No, I just came to support the marathon. I was a volunteer at last night's Rendezvous."

"I'm not supposed to let anyone in that isn't here on official police business, but I can at least tell you. The viewing stand collapsed. They think there was someone under it."

The viewing stand? Wasn't that the structure Terry Seiser claimed he'd been working on? "That's horrible. Do they know who it was?"

She shook her head. "I just got here a little while ago. All I know is that it wasn't a runner."

My phone rang. She allowed me to pull off to the side to answer it.

"Did I interrupt your beauty sleep?" Herc asked, his typical way of greeting me when he called early in the morning. He knew better because I'm still an early riser, a habit that carried over from my days on the force.

"There are so many possible replies to that question, but I think I've exhausted them over the years. What's up?"

"Funny you should ask. Actually, not funny. That guy that disrupted things last night, Seiser?"

"Yes?" I replied, my fingers tingling, knowing what was to come.

"He was in an accident here at the marathon. The whole viewing stand collapsed on top of him. They just pulled out the body."

CHAPTER 4

"If it was an accident, why are you there, Herc?" It was a Saturday morning, time he usually claimed as his duty-free zone unless something really big was going on. I was pretty sure I knew the answer to my question already, but I wanted verification.

"The guy was Al Buford, Herc's partner's cousin. Maybe not kissin' cousins, but they called Al as the next of kin. Al called me before he even got here. Said his cousin may have been a jerk to most people, but the guy knew his product, especially when he was using it to build the viewing stand. He couldn't prove it yet, but he suspected funny business had caused the cave-in."

"Why did you call me?" I asked.

"Al asked me to. If the death is suspicious, he wants you to help me investigate. He's too close to it."

A thousand different thoughts ran through my brain. Al actually wanted me involved? He really had to be concerned his cousin had been killed to want me on the case. If Seiser had been killed, who did it? The last person he'd fought with was Shane Bolton. Surely Shane wouldn't have let his anger get away from him? But there'd been over fifty witnesses to their brawl. His name was sure to come up first.

"As it turns out, I'm already here at the park. I came to observe the race. How do I find you?"

"I'll send someone to bring you over. Leave your car where it is for now."

Five minutes later, I stood with Herc and Al observing the collapsed viewing stand from a distance. The medical team had already left with the body after a brief review by the medical examiner. The forensics team was still taking measurements and photos. There was very little we could do other than take in the details of the disaster.

"Thanks for coming, Ro," Al said in all sincerity. "Terry was a real pill, but we were still family. He deserves the best figuring out what happened and who did it." He didn't exactly say that was me, but for Al, that was a huge vote of confidence.

Put that way, I couldn't very well refuse to help even though I'd already held off putting my finishing touches on Mehaffy House and had done very little to prepare for Christmas and New Year's.

In my hesitation, Herc filled in. "Can you help us, Ro? I know you've already put off work on your rehab project to help me catch the killer at that modeling agency, but Al really wants the two of us to handle this."

Al hadn't exactly endeared himself to me since becoming Herc's new partner, and Terry Seiser certainly was no friend of mine, but everyone deserved a fair review when it came to finding their killer.

I released a long sigh before replying. "Before I agree to help, tell me why you suspect foul play rather than a tragic accident, Al."

"I can't think of any good reason why my cousin would go under that platform. If he'd been anywhere else when the thing caved in, like standing on top of it or leaning on one of the sides, he might've been hurt. But he wouldn't have been killed barring additional circumstances."

I wasn't convinced. Al was in shock and, in that condition, was attempting to make sense of the unexplained. Didn't Herc realize this? Probably, and not wanting to disappoint his partner, was turning to me to be the voice of reason. "Herc said the medical examiner had been here. Did he have anything to say about the condition of the, uh, body?" Perhaps too direct, but the only way I knew to steer us through this situation.

Al bit his lip, tears coming to his eyes. "Yes and no. He was, uh, pretty banged up. Even his phone was damaged beyond repair. Dr. Kelsey was hesitant to voice any opinion other than Terry was dead. Why do you ask?"

"If you believe there was no way your cousin would've gone underneath the stand, yet he was still found there, the only way he could've gotten there was to have been dragged there against his will. Most likely he would have been knocked unconscious to get him underneath. If that was the case, there should be some sign on his body of being physically overcome."

"Good point, Ro. He could've been bashed on the head, drugged or injected with something." Herc turned to Al. "If Doc Kelsey finds anything like that, then you're right. This was a homicide. But until then …?"

"But Herc …" Al said plaintively.

Uncharacteristically, Herc planted a hand on his partner's shoulder. "Look, man, you've had a lot to take in at this early hour of the morning. Give Ro and me a chance to look around, see what we can see. You go home and get some rest. There's nothing you can do until we know more from the ME."

"Rest?" Al wasn't exactly screaming, but clearly he wasn't going along with Herc's suggestion. "There's no way I could sleep. Not after all this happened."

"Then don't sleep," Herc replied, attempting to placate him. "But go home. Eat something. At least have some coffee. Watch some mindless TV if nothing else. Since you're his next-of-kin, you'll have plenty to do within a day, making, uh, arrangements. Before then, call the captain and ask for bereavement leave."

"Take time off? I may need a day or two for a funeral and all that, but I need to work right now. I know I can't handle this case, as much as I'd like to, but I can't stay home twiddling my thumbs, letting whatever happened here run loops in my brain."

"I know that will be difficult," I said. "I certainly had difficulties making it through my grief after my husband died. It didn't come out of the blue, as happened here with your cousin, but that didn't make it hurt any less. Take this a day at a time. Herc and I will look into this disaster and determine if there's cause to see it as anything other than an accident. Those are my terms, if you want me in on this."

Too harsh? I didn't think so. The man was functioning on pure adrenaline right now. His emotions could take him anywhere. He needed to withdraw from this reality and focus on moving ahead. And my usually tough-as-nails ex-partner appeared to be a blob of jelly at the moment. He wasn't up to it.

Blinking, Al took a step back and ran a hand through his hair. "You're right, Ro. If this happened to anyone else, I'd be telling them the same. I'll make a deal with you. If you two will call me later after you've had time to study things and keep me in the loop, I'll go home now. Can't guarantee I'll sleep, but I'll have the bowl of cereal I missed when I got the call about Terry."

"It's a deal," I replied before Herc had a chance to react.

"Thanks, Ro," Herc said once Al was out of earshot. "You knew exactly what to say."

"Part of me was hoping I'd come on too strong and he wouldn't want me on the case any longer. Looks like for now, at least, I judged wrong."

"You don't think it was murder, do you?" he asked.

"I don't know with a certainty it was murder. The guy I met just days ago was full of himself. That kind often takes chances they shouldn't because they think they're invulnerable."

"Yeah, I got that impression last night. Any idea why he showed up like he did?"

"Offhand, without knowing him any better than from my recent run-in with him, I'd say he was there to make a statement of some sort, or he would've arrived through the front like everyone else and mixed with the rest of the crowd, keeping a low profile."

"From what little I observed, seems like that statement was aimed at your boy, Shane Bolton."

I'd been afraid Shane's name would pop up, sooner or later. It came up much sooner than I hoped. "There was bad blood between the two men, but not so bad Shane would follow Seiser here and kill him."

Herc gave me one of those "get real" looks he saved for times like this when I went too far out on a limb. Experience had taught me that almost anyone was capable of terrible acts if provoked enough, so if Seiser had been killed, we couldn't dismiss Shane as a suspect. At least not until we talked to him and hopefully got a rock-solid alibi.

First, I needed to get the lay of the land. Since I wasn't into running marathons, I wanted to know where the now-defunct viewing stand was located in relation to the rest of the race. It was just over the finish line. Apparently they planned to award the medals there. I could only guess what it must've looked like a few hours ago. Now it was a pile of lumber. There was no way to picture what it looked like after it had fallen, because much of it had been thrown aside to get to Seiser. But there was so much of it, it didn't take much to imagine how it could crush the life out of a human being.

There appeared to be tire tracks about ten feet away from the pile, but they weren't clear. Probably disturbed by first responders trampling over them to rescue Seiser.

"Pretty crappy ending to a life, even someone like Seiser," Herc said, coming up to me as I stood there attempting to picture how such a tragedy could happen.

"Did Seiser leave any of his things behind?" I asked.

"Not that we can tell. If anything was left up on top of the platform, it's part of that rubble now. His pickup is parked not too far away, if you want to search it?"

"Yeah, I do, if the forensics team has finished reviewing it?"

"They're done. Go ahead. What are you looking for?"

"The plans he was using to construct the stand. More than likely he had them with him as he must've done a last-minute once-over of the thing this morning, but just in case he left them in the pickup, we need to find out."

As it turned out, plans of some sort had been left on the front seat. Hands gloved, without touching anything else in the cab, I retrieved the documents and went off to a nearby park bench to study them. Was it his vehicle that had made the tracks near the collapsed platform?

"Those tell you anything?" Herc asked, approaching me.

"Apparently it was a flat platform, twelve by ten feet built seven feet above ground with steps going up to it on one end. That's about all I can glean from this overview. There should've been more detailed schematics illustrating how everything was put together. I'm guessing those went with him to the stand and are probably buried inside that wreckage."

"There'll be a crew out here in the next few days to haul off all that debris. Maybe they'll come across the plans when they do."

"That's a pretty big maybe, but I won't dismiss the possibility entirely. I didn't note anything else that might shine some light on this situation when I searched the cab of his pickup, but you never know. Will the truck be impounded while the case is open?"

"I haven't done anything official yet, but I will. It's the only physical evidence we have, other than what might be back at the lumberyard or his house."

Since there was a bit of a breeze, I circumnavigated the disaster zone, searching the ground. Maybe, just maybe, the wind had made off with the rest of the plans. A girl could hope, although as it turned out, my aspirations were a bit too optimistic. We found nothing related to Seiser.

At length, I turned to Herc, finished with my mission. "I'm done here. How about you?"

"Yeah. I was done before you got here, especially since the

forensics team took a million photos of the scene. What do you suggest we do next while we wait to hear from the ME?"

"Is that a cry for caffeine?" I asked.

"Actually, I was wondering if we should head into the station and rehash what we've learned or go to your place and do the same there. But if you want to stop off somewhere for coffee and doughnuts, I won't object."

CHAPTER 5

We'd barely consumed our containers of coffee when Herc received a call from Whip Kelsey, the ME. We went outside, where Herc put him on speaker.

"I was seventy-five percent sure of my findings from the cursory examination I did at the accident scene, but I wanted to be absolutely sure, especially because your partner was so close to the victim. But I wasn't wrong. He'd clearly been hit on the back of the head with a heavy object. That didn't kill him, but it did leave him unconscious so he could be dragged under the platform. That much was evident, even though the drag marks had been cleared way. There were bits of grass and dirt in his hair as well as on the back of his shirt and trousers."

"So it was murder," Herc said.

"Yes, but not from the blow to his head," Kelsey replied. "That simply disabled him. It was the impact of the collapse of the platform that did him in. He died both from head trauma and a crushed chest, which disabled his heart."

"Any idea what caused the collapse?" Herc asked.

"Sorry, Herc. All I can do is confirm it was a homicide. How it happened, I can't determine from the state of the body. That's up to you and your team."

"Thanks for getting back to me so fast, Doc. Especially on the weekend."

"All I can offer you right now is this preliminary report. The full autopsy will take a few more days. I'll email what I've got to you, then I'm off for a late round of golf. I leave the rest of the detecting to you."

Herc clicked off and turned back to me. "That's what I was afraid of. Someone caused that platform to fall, not something easily done, especially in a matter of minutes before someone else came along and spotted them. Besides determining how they did it, we need to know who and why."

Easily stated, but answering those three questions was not going to be easy. "I suggest we start with the who by having Al provide us with a list of those persons closest to the victim. Do you think he'll be able to talk yet?" I asked.

"I doubt he's past the shock, but he'd want to be consulted as soon as possible, now that we know it was murder," Herc said. He snarfed down the rest of his doughnut as we headed for his car.

Al appeared at the door of his apartment, having changed to board shorts and a loose-fitting tee. His eyes were red-rimmed, his nose dripping.

"Sorry to disturb you, bud," Herc said, "but we thought you'd want to know the results as soon as we knew."

Al motioned for us to come into his small but tidy living room. The only sign of human occupation was an open box of cinnamon rolls and a large container of water. "It was murder, wasn't it?" he asked before we were even seated.

I let Herc handle this part. He knew best how to handle his partner. "Yes, man, it was as you suspected. Doc Kelsey confirmed he was struck on the head, knocked unconscious and then dragged under the platform. Whoever did the deed covered up the drag marks on the ground, but they didn't get the grass and dirt out of his hair or the back of his clothes."

Al just sat there for several seconds, his hands folded, looking down. At last he spoke. "Thanks for coming to tell me in person. I'm still having difficulty believing he's gone."

"You know what we tell the loved ones and friends of other victims, to take your time to work through your grief, that the feelings you're experiencing won't go away overnight," Herc said. Over the years, I'd seen him be extremely thoughtful and kind when handling those dealing with the aftermath of murder, but he was even more understanding with Al.

"I hear what you're saying. It's just surreal."

"We're gonna find whoever did this," Herc told him. "In fact, that's partially why we're here. We thought you'd know best who might fit that bill."

"I figured you'd want to know that, if it did turn out to be homicide. I've been making a list in my head. There aren't many names. Terry wasn't much of a social animal."

That was putting it mildly, although I didn't say so.

"Was he married?" Herc asked.

"At one time, but that was years ago. She left him and remarried. I heard through the grapevine that she passed away five years ago. No kids. No brothers or sisters. I was his closest kin. Our dads were brothers."

Time for me to get involved. "Did he live alone?"

"He had a live-in housekeeper. After his wife left, he didn't pay much attention to keeping the place up. I couldn't believe how he'd trashed it when I visited him some time later. I convinced him he either had to start caring more about the upkeep or hire someone to handle that for him. I recommended this woman I'd run into during one of my early cases. She took the job and has stayed with him ever since. Her name is Carmen Loomis."

Herc and I made note of the name. "How about his business?" I asked. "Do you know anyone there?"

"I don't know anyone at the lumberyard, but there's this woman who's been his bookkeeper for years. Muriel Fox. She'd be able to help you with the names of other staff and clients."

"Anyone else?" Herc asked.

Al shook his head. "Sorry. We weren't all that close, especially the last twenty years or so. As you'll learn from these two women, if they're honest, and whoever else you talk to, Terry wasn't the most agreeable of people. I don't know if it was his wife leaving him or if it goes back even further to his parents, although his dad, Bill, was a great guy. His personality must've grated on someone so much they wanted him dead."

"How did you find out about the accident, uh, collapse of the platform?" I asked.

"Terry called me out of the blue a few days ago and invited me to stop by and see it. I hadn't heard him so excited in some time. He's never been one to get involved in community-type stuff like the marathon. I've no idea what got him interested in this event. I got there at the same time the first responders were arriving. I didn't know it was him until they pulled him out of that wreckage, although I suspected as much when I didn't see him anywhere."

"I'm sorry you had to learn of his death that way," I said. No one should have to learn of the death of a family member like that.

"Thanks, Ro. I never imagined he'd go the way he did."

Herc rose. Even though this was his partner, he could only take so much sentiment. He was anxious to get started. "We'll let you be. You've got a lot of details to work through. You know the drill. Call if you think of anything else that might help our investigation."

Al got up and came with us to the door. "Thanks again for personally handling this case, both of you."

Herc and I didn't speak for several beats once back in his car. He was taking the death of his partner's cousin more seriously than he'd let on to Al. I was less affected that way, although I did feel for Al, but I was reviewing what little information we'd gleaned from Al and realizing we had a long road ahead of us. Al was trained to absorb a lot of details in his work as a homicide detective, and yet he'd only been able to share a few details with us. Was that from shock, or was there really that little to know?

Plus, how would we deal with the elephant in the room, er, car? Shane Bolton. As far as we knew, Shane was the last person to have words with Seiser. Words that had almost come to blows, which were only deflected by Henson and Herc. As much as I didn't want to talk about Shane with Herc right now, my better cop sense told me finding Shane was the most critical item on our plate right now.

"Okay, Ro. I've given you a little time to switch from accident to homicide scenarios. You know as well as I do what our next step is, who we have to talk to first."

"Shane Bolton," I said with very little enthusiasm.

"Do you want to call him, or would you prefer I do it in my professional capacity?"

"I'll do it. I know how bad it looks for him, but I just can't believe he would do such a thing."

"You know the rules of investigation, Ro. You can't take anything for granted."

"I know. Maybe I should recuse myself from this case too. Like Al, I seem to be personally involved."

"Oh, no you don't. We've known other suspects over the years, and you've always been absolutely scrupulous in the way you related to them."

"I was just offering you the option to pull in one of your junior staff instead of me. If you think I'm leaning too much in his favor, the offer still stands."

He heaved a breath. "Fine. I'll keep that in mind. But for now, let's find Bolton."

We started at The Sandpiper. "Sorry, guys. I can't help," Chuck replied when we asked after Shane. "He never came back last night and didn't show up this morning. And he's not answering his phone. I've already left a couple messages." He jotted something down on a notepad and handed it to me. Shane's address and phone number. "Good luck. I hope you find him. Disappearing right now doesn't look good."

No, it didn't, although I didn't need to say as much out loud.

"Any idea where he might be if not at his apartment?" I asked.

Chuck made a face. Trying to think or trying to deflect the question? "The guy's pretty close-mouthed about his private life, but you might try contacting that real estate agent friend of Val's. The two of them appeared to have something going not too long back."

"Amanda Casey?" I replied.

"Yeah, she's the one. Remember how she glommed onto him when we first opened?"

I thought back to that event. Chuck and I were already seeing each other exclusively at that point, but he hadn't moved in yet. Amanda had seemed interested in Chuck's good-looking manager that night, but after that, I recalled how she roped Val and me into being her wing ladies when she had a blind date at a local wine bar. That's when Chuck got the idea to open his own.

"Has Shane been seeing her lately? She didn't attend the Rendezvous last night."

Chuck raised his shoulders. "Ask Val. She'd know more than me."

"You're right," I agreed. "I'll give her a call if we haven't located him."

Herc and I took our leave and headed toward the address Chuck gave us. Despite trying to maintain a neutral attitude, I couldn't help hoping he hadn't done anything stupid, like run, and that we'd find him at home.

CHAPTER 6

Shane lived in a small, older apartment building two blocks from The Sandpiper. Herc and I stood for some time in his hallway after knocking before he came to the door. I'd almost been ready to give up.

"Figured you'd show up sooner or later," he said to Herc.

"That why you haven't been answering your phone?" Herc fired back.

"I took a long bike ride. Ever since I heard about Seiser's death on the news, I've been in a state of flux. My first reaction was shock. As much as part of me might've wanted that outcome last night, my better sense knew that was just a gut reaction to his baiting me."

"Are you sure that bike ride didn't take you through Busse Park *before* you heard the news?" Herc asked none too subtly.

Shane narrowed his eyes. "Yes. Why would you even ask me that?"

"Don't play dumb with us, Bolton," Herc replied. "I helped break up your fight with Seiser before you were ready to quit. Then you ran off and didn't return to the restaurant the rest of the evening. Who's to say you didn't relive the incident in your head all night and decide to confront him again this morning? You knew exactly where he'd be at that time and probably figured he'd be there alone."

Shane straightened his shoulders. "If you're suggesting I had anything to do with his accident, you're wrong. Last night's encounter really threw me. I thought I was over all those feelings a long time ago, but the ease with which the guy got under my skin unnerved me. Enough that I forgot all about work this morning. Didn't even call Chuck to tell him I was running behind. That's not like me. But, no, I did not seek him out this morning for a second round."

The tension between the two men had quickly escalated. It wasn't like Herc to go for the jugular quite so soon with a suspect, or in this case, person of interest. Was he that sure Shane was guilty, or was he trying to shake him? Though Herc might not appreciate it, it was time for me to intercede and lighten things up a bit. "What's going on, Shane? You're always so cool reacting to hostile parties. Just the other day, you didn't let Daryl Henson get to you when he started throwing his perceived security weight around. What was there about Seiser?"

Shane gestured for us to enter the room and take seats. He settled in a chair across from us. "I told you most of the story last week after your run-in with him, Ro. I worked at Seiser's Hardware and Lumberyard when I was a teen. Bill Seiser was still alive then. We got along great. Once or twice, he mentioned training me for a leadership role in the business someday. Terry was the typical screwup as a teen, getting in trouble with the law several times. Nothing serious. He didn't deal well with rules."

I made a mental note to check Seiser's past history with the law.

"Bill would probably never have suggested a future for me in the business if Terry had shown any kind of interest or ability. Terry just assumed since he was the only child that the business would come to him someday. He didn't like his dad paying more attention to me. He did everything he could to get me fired. He finally succeeded when he claimed I'd stolen cash from the register. I didn't, but Bill didn't have any recourse but to let me go."

"So you've been harboring this grudge against him ever since," Herc said, pouncing on that last part.

Shane held up a hand. "No, it wasn't like that. Not exactly, anyhow. Getting fired turned out to be one of the best things that ever happened to me. Had I stayed on, I would've gotten too comfortable with the work and never tried for anything else. Instead, I went to college and got my degree in business management. That led to a job as manager in a Serendipity Springs supper club, and then I applied for the same type of work at The Sandpiper. While I was in college, I ran into Bill, who promptly apologized for letting me go. He'd since learned that I was innocent and had tried to get in touch with me to offer my old job back but had been unable to find me."

He needn't have said more; we were getting the picture. But this discourse seemed to be lightening the tension, and I wasn't ready to let it die down. "Did Bill Seiser admit it had been Terry who set you up?"

"Not in so many words. But we both knew what happened. I'd heard through the grapevine that Bill was suffering from COPD. He didn't look well at that time. When I think about it now, it had probably dawned on him that if the business was to continue after he was gone, it all depended on Terry."

"But that was years ago," Herc said, changing his stance enough to participate in this discussion. "Didn't you get past whatever bad feelings you had for him?"

Shane released a long sigh. "I thought so. Even when you, Ro, told me about his immediate refusal to donate to the event, I was pretty cool about it. Remember? I was still cool when he showed up unexpectedly through the back entrance last night. It was only when he started bragging about his connection to Ellen Garvey and his major role in the marathon that something snapped."

Herc looked up. "Snapped?"

"No, forget I said that. What I meant was I'd been trying so hard to expand my role in the community by working on this event. I couldn't believe Terry had gotten himself associated with it too. What was he up to? Because there had to be something in it for him. Even as I was taking a swing at him, I knew it was wrong. I'm so glad you guys stopped me. But I was also embarrassed that he still had that effect on me. I had to get out of there. I didn't sleep much through the night. I kept wondering what he was up to. How had he worked himself into the role of community supporter? That was so not him. Terry Seiser only cared about Terry Seiser."

I was almost buying his story. Almost. Even he had noted that his reaction to Seiser didn't happen immediately. Something Seiser said had triggered Shane's violent response. Did that response continue to fester and grow through the night to the point Shane was compelled to have it out with him this morning?

Time to set him straight about the accident. "You're probably wondering why the two of us are here to talk about the *accident*," I said.

Shane stared me down. "It wasn't an accident, was it? This is an official police visit following a homicide. Thanks to losing it last night, I guess that puts me at the top or near the top of your list of suspects."

He sounded so calm, but from the way his right index finger was rubbing his thumb, he was anything but calm.

"Bingo," Herc said. "You've already given us your side of what happened last night and why you fled the event. You also said you didn't sleep much because you kept thinking about the man and that you took off on a bike ride this morning rather than reporting to work or even notifying your employer you weren't coming in. Want to change any of that now?"

Shane remained quiet. Thinking through his statements? More like realizing how bad things looked for him. "Are you here to arrest me?"

"Not yet," Herc replied. "We still have a few more details to check. But you can see how things look for you."

Shane lowered his head and eyed his hands. "Yeah, I do. But I didn't kill him. I didn't go near the park this morning."

"If you didn't kill him, can you think of anyone else who might have done him in?" I asked.

"I haven't had anything to do with him since I left the business, although I've occasionally heard things about him. If you're serious about considering other suspects, look either to the business, which rumor has it has been losing money ever since Bill died, or talk to the women in his life. I don't know how he did it, being such a grump and not much to look at, but I've heard he's seen more than one woman since his marriage tanked. Maybe even Ellen Garvey. That might explain how he got himself such a cushy job with the marathon."

Ellen Garvey? I didn't know her well, but she came across as so in control and sophisticated. Not the type I'd think would give Terry Seiser a second glance. But Shane had a point. How had Seiser gotten himself involved in a community event without someone like Ellen's help?

"What do you know about his marriage?" Herc asked.

"Nothing more than I just told you. It went bust, years ago. Maybe twenty? I'd just set out on my own and heard about the marriage from customers I knew from the hardware store. Maybe over a year later, former customers told me about the breakup. Didn't surprise me at all. Seiser didn't get along with many people. What surprised me was the fact some woman married him in the first place."

"Do you know the woman's name?" I asked.

Shane shook his head. "No. Talk to the woman who essentially runs the hardware store and lumberyard, Muriel Fox. She's probably your best source of information about his business and private life."

Herc gave him the usual spiel about letting us know if he thought of anything else and if he left town, to let us know.

Had we learned much from Shane? He contended he didn't kill Seiser, but he didn't have an alibi for his whereabouts from the time he took off from the Rendezvous until we'd shown up at his door.

Herc asked another question. "When was the last time you rode your bike, Bolton?"

Shane cocked his head. "I don't know. Does it matter?"

"Take a guess. In the last week? In the last month? Or last several months?" I assumed he was trying ascertain if this morning's bike ride was out of the ordinary, and if so, why.

Shane shifted his weight. "I can't really say. I ride it every so often, but I haven't had much free time lately, so it's been weeks at least."

That led to one more question from Herc. "Where'd you go on your ride?"

"I can't really say where I went. Wherever seven to ten thirty would take me." Then he caught Herc's studied gaze. "Once again, I did not go into or anywhere near Busse Park, if that's what you're thinking."

"You just told me you weren't sure where you went. How can you be so sure you weren't in or near the park?"

"I was still embarrassed by my actions last night. I didn't want to be anywhere near where anyone in attendance last night would see me."

Herc continued to eye him suspiciously, apparently thinking he could stare an admission out of Shane. Not happening. Shane clammed up at that point, so we took our leave.

CHAPTER 7

The first thing I did once I was in the car again was call Chuck. "You're about thirty seconds behind Shane," Chuck said. "After he apologized for his behavior last night and for not calling right away today, he told me he wasn't coming in today, that is, if I could spare him. I really can't, but from his tone, he needs time away."

"Uh, yeah. Did he mention we'd determined that Seiser was murdered, it wasn't an accident, and Shane's at the top of our suspect list?"

"Yes. He also strongly claimed he didn't do it. You don't really think he did, do you? This is Shane. We both know him. He's one of the good guys."

"That's what I'd like to continue to think," I replied. "But we both witnessed his anger last night. He would've mixed it up big time with the man had he not been restrained. It didn't help that he immediately ran off and has no alibi for that time until we found him this morning."

"We? Are you teamed up with Morgan again?"

I did a mental head kick. I should've called him sooner. He wasn't crazy about the amount of time I spent investigating homicides when that was what put me into a serious vehicle accident and ended my ongoing field career. I didn't think it was because he was jealous. He was really looking out for my welfare. But since things had gotten serious between the two of us recently, he deserved to know right away that I was back on a case again.

"Yes. As it turns out, Herc's partner, Al Buford, was the victim's cousin and his closest next-of-kin. He not only recused himself from the case because he'd be too close to it, he specifically asked me to join Herc. Despite the fact I was just coming off the Craddock case, I didn't feel I could let him down."

"I get that, Ro. It's just terrible timing. I've been looking forward to spending the better part of the holidays with you. Christmas shopping, picking out a tree."

"We'll do that and more, Chuck. Just give me a couple days to wrap this case."

He didn't respond to my statement. I wish he would've gotten angry, slammed down the phone, anything but the silent treatment.

"Chuck? I mean it."

"Yeah, I know. I've got plenty to do here at the restaurant and wine bar today." His tone was that of resignation and deep disappointment.

Something told me if I kept attempting to apologize, I'd make it even worse. I pretended to take his last statement in stride. "Okay, see you sometime later today. Thanks for understanding."

I knew as soon as that last part was said, I'd made matters even worse.

"Even I know you went too far with that last bit," Herc said after I hung up. "I get his frustration. I called Luann a little while ago to beg off the shopping day she had planned for us. She, too, put up a brave front, but I could tell I was in the doghouse."

"I shouldn't have to feel so guilty, Herc. I'm doing something noble. I'm helping Al and the city by agreeing to find Seiser's killer."

"The two of us have been lone rangers too long. We're used to putting our cases front and foremost. Now that we both have others in our lives, we need to keep reminding ourselves we've got someone else who needs to be kept in the loop more than either of us has done in the past."

I swiveled to look at him. "Who are you? I've always been the reasonable one in our partnership."

"Just sayin'. You and Deli Man have to work out your own ways of keeping each other informed. Being public safety herself, Luann probably understands better than your guy that murders don't take place on our schedules."

"Point taken. Let's see how many suspects we can get to today."

"WELL, WELL. LOOK WHO FINALLY SHOWED UP ON MY DOORSTEP," Daryl Henson said when he came to the door of his condo.

"Daryl, mind if Ro and I come to chat with you about your role in the Reindeer Run?" Herc asked in an unusually civil tone for him.

With a sweeping gesture of his hand, the former vice cop showed us into his home. The faint aroma of garlic permeated the room, more than likely something at least two days old. Probably takeout.

His living room was a hodgepodge of furniture styles. A maroon plaid sectional hugged two walls. A hunter green leather recliner, too big for the room, occupied another corner in the place of honor facing a huge flat-screen TV across from it. Two other easy chairs, one light blue, one off-white, fought for the remaining space. We'd run across him earlier in the year when we'd investigated a murder in the building. He'd just moved in after selling his former home when he retired from the force. It appeared he'd brought all his old furniture with him.

"I take it you haven't caught whoever killed Terry Seiser yet," he said, true to form, taking the lead in the conversation in an attempt to control whatever was said. Herc and I were both on to his tactic.

"That murder shouldn't have ever occurred, if there'd been proper security surrounding the event," Herc said, fully knowing those were fighting words with this man.

Henson's whole face turned red, and his eyes appeared about to pop. I swore his head swelled up, like air being pumped into a bicycle tire. "For once, we agree on something, Morgan. Only don't pin the blame on me. I did everything in my power to wake them up to the risks they faced if they didn't pay more attention to security."

"Are you talking about the event committee or the city parks people?" I asked.

"Both, but mainly the committee. They saw my role mainly as crowd control and coordinating traffic. Important, but not enough. The park people thought the few cameras they had in place were more than enough. Bet they'll change their tune now."

"Are you saying that, until the day of the event, no precautions were taken to safeguard the race route?" Herc asked.

"You got it. I should've known I'd signed up with a kindergarten operation that first time I met with that charlatan Milligan. His primary item of business was to demand he be assigned the parking spot closest to the entrance. Forget about the mayor or the sponsors. No, he needed immediate access to the course that morning."

"Milligan? Who's he?" Herc asked.

"Cyrus Milligan, supposed marathon consultant. I don't know where they got him. Wouldn't even glance at my security plan when I handed it to him. Tossed it, tossed it, mind you, onto the back seat of his car when we first met. That was another thing. Couldn't even meet in an office or restaurant. He only had time in his 'busy' schedule to catch me in the parking lot of a gym downtown. That, along with the parking spot thing, should've tipped me off this wasn't gonna end pretty."

"What happened to the security plan?" I asked. Henson might

be a dirty cop, an as yet unproved dirty cop because Herc and I hadn't been able to pin anything on him when he was on active duty, but I had to give him his due. He surely knew enough police procedure to write a decent plan. Although I couldn't speak to his spelling and grammar. And ability to write complete sentences.

Henson's countenance had returned to the same pasty level as when he'd opened the door. "I went to the top dog, Ellen Garvey. She had no idea who I was. Apparently it was her money man who told her she had to include a security expert. She handed off the task to Milligan. No idea how he found me. My luck, huh?"

This was fast turning into Henson's pity party. We didn't have time to massage his ego. We needed to get on with this investigation before the trail got any colder. "As for Ellen Garvey," I said, attempting to get us back on track, "what did she say about the security plan?"

"Didn't know a thing about it. Milligan never showed it to her. That's how much importance they placed on security."

"Did Milligan ever get back to you about the plan?" Herc asked.

"Not until I tracked him down at a nail spa. I'm still pretty good at birddogging. He couldn't remember who I was. When I explained I needed the go-ahead to set my recommendations in motion, he just stared at me. When I pushed for his approval, he said fine, just don't spend any money and stay out of the park until the day of the race."

"How'd you react to those instructions?" I asked. If security hadn't been such a key factor in Seiser's death, Henson's dilemma with his new bosses would've been comical. But his situation was nothing to laugh about.

"Went to the rest of the planning committee. Found out when they were meeting and showed up without an invite. They gave me five minutes to make my pitch. When I finished, they nodded politely, gave lip service to the need for good security and then dismissed me. I'd gone ready to demand a seat at the table but never got that far. I had to be content with text updates to Milligan."

"You never got near the viewing platform?" Herc asked.

"Tried, more than once, but Seiser caught me, even when I was surveilling his work from a nearby stand of trees. Accused me of spying for the committee. What a laugh. They were the last ones who wanted me there."

I caught Herc's head nod, imperceptible to the rest of humankind. We wouldn't be getting much more information from Henson other than additional poor-me statements. Time to leave the man licking his wounds.

Our next stop was the victim's business, Seiser's Hardware Store and Lumberyard.

We seemed to be the only people in the place other than the young kid lounging behind the counter. "Sorry, we're closed due to the death of the owner."

"Oh? The front door's not locked," Herc replied.

"Right. I was on my way there when you walked in."

"Getting directions from your phone?" I asked.

"As a matter of fact, I was. From the office manager. She didn't come in today."

"Muriel Fox, right?" Herc asked.

"Yeah. She took the day off to help at the marathon."

Herc showed his badge. The kid glanced at it but didn't appear impressed from the way he continued to slouch over the counter, not putting down his phone.

"We need her address then," I said.

"How come? Did she cause the accident?" Now the kid was interested.

I waited to see if Herc would tell him his boss had been murdered. "We're following up on the incident," was all he said.

"Do you know anything about the contraption he was building as a viewing stand?"

The kid snickered. "You mean all the lumber he's been hauling out to the park the past few days? I just work here part-time, so I don't see him all that much, which is just fine with me, but I've never seen him so full of himself. Like he thought he'd be crowned citizen of the year."

It appeared we'd run into another member of the Terry Seiser Fan Club. I slid a glance at Herc and caught his subtle nod. Might as well milk this kid's impression of Seiser since we were here. "Sounds like you weren't a fan of your boss," I said.

"It's a job, and I need the money. Not the same physical grind as my friends who work at the big box stores. I let his attitude roll off me as much as I could."

"What's your name, kid? And how long have you worked here?" Herc asked.

The kid's eyes darted from Herc to me. Would we learn something about him he didn't want us to know if we got his name? "Karl. Karl Backstrom. I got hired about three weeks ago. The kid who worked here before got fired. Don't know why, and Seiser didn't want to talk about it."

"What did you mean by Mr. Seiser's 'attitude'?" I asked.

He shot a look at his phone but put it down. Didn't want to mess with the police? "He was always angry. Nothing seemed to satisfy him. Found fault with any little thing. If it weren't for Muriel, I woulda left long ago. After Seiser lit into me the first time for absolutely nothing, she waited till the guy was out of hearing and then told me not to take him seriously. Well, I had to take instructions seriously, but no matter what I did, Seiser didn't praise me."

"You seem like a smart enough kid, Karl," I said, appealing to his ego, "so how would you describe the atmosphere around here lately?"

"Atmosphere? You mean like was it a fun place to work? That's a definite no. But the guy seemed preoccupied the last week or so. He wasn't exactly happy, but this thing he was doing for the marathon seemed to make him a little less negative. I mentioned it to Muriel one day. She agreed he was somewhat less angry than usual, so just stay out of his way and not wreck his mood."

"Was anyone else working on the viewing stand with him?" Herc asked.

Karl considered the question, then shook his head. "Not that I know of. No one popped in and acted like they were part of things. And from what little I know of the guy, he wasn't one to work with a partner."

"Did he leave any plans for the viewing stand lying around here?" I asked, ninety-nine percent sure he hadn't.

"Not that I saw. But then, I don't know if I woulda recognized plans like that anyhow."

Herc handed him his card. "If you do find anything that might have been the plans, get in touch with me. Or if anything else of note occurs to you."

"Okay."

"We still need contact information for Ms. Fox," I said before we left.

Karl grabbed a pen and paper and jotted something on it. "I wouldn't normally know how to reach her, except she left this with me since I would be on my own today," he said, handing it over.

At the door, Herc turned back. "Better lock up after us, since that's what you've been instructed to do."

"Uh, yeah, sure."

"How much do you want to bet the kid invites his pals to stop by while he's got the run of the place?" Herc asked on our way to the car.

"Possibly, since he didn't appear to move after you reminded him about the door. I'm glad you didn't just turn around and walk out when we learned the Fox woman wasn't there. We gleaned a little more background about Seiser."

"I wonder if Seiser knew that kid would be the only one covering the store today," Herc said. "His letting that happen doesn't wash with everything else we've been hearing about him. And what's the deal with the lumberyard? Does it function as a separate entity?"

"Do you want to stop by there?"

"Not yet, although I'm guessing Seiser procured all his materials from his own stock. I'd like an inventory of what he took. But I suspect Muriel Fox would be the best source of that data."

"Let's go talk to her," I said, "and catch her before her shock wears off and she starts revising history."

"What makes you think she'd do that?"

"From what Karl told us about her, I'm guessing she's been playing mediator between Seiser and the rest of the world for some time."

I handed Herc the address and telephone number Karl had given me. Herc entered the info into the GPS, and we took off.

I hoped Muriel Fox could fill in a lot of the blanks about her boss.

CHAPTER 8

"Before we talk to this Fox woman," Herc said, "I need your opinion on something."

"Okay? About that shirt? Yellow isn't your best color, but it works."

He made a face. "Really? I wear this shirt all the time."

"I'm sure it's comfortable or you wouldn't wear it so often. And comfort counts a lot when you're into a big investigation."

"Good theory, but I didn't know I'd be looking into another homicide when I got dressed this morning. I'll change before I see Luann tonight."

After all these years, my partner was considering his wardrobe. Things must have progressed faster with Luann than he was letting on.

"Speaking of Luann, uh, that's where I need your opinion. As another woman, you know?"

What was going on here? So far in his relationship with the assistant fire inspector, Herc had been very reluctant to discuss the new woman in his life. I braced for whatever question or comment was to come. "What about Luann?"

He fiddled with his shirt collar before replying. "I sorta wish we'd started seeing each other several months ago or after the middle of February. At this point, everything's so new and all, I don't know how far to go with a Christmas gift."

Though tempted to laugh at his uncertainty or kid him about it, I restrained myself. He was serious. I took a shot at responding to his dilemma. "Your question is, what should you get her?"

"Stupid, huh? I suppose I could get by with candy or flowers, or candy and flowers. But neither feels right."

"Candy and flowers are almost always fine, unless she's on a diet or diabetic or allergic to either one. What it sounds like you're asking is how big a gift to give this early in your friendship."

"Yeah, I knew you'd catch on fast."

"What do you want to give her? Has she hinted at anything?"

"Luann? No, she's not the type. Or if she is, I've been too obtuse to pick up on her signals."

"You haven't shared much about how things are progressing between the two of you, but my intuition tells me it might be too early for anything expensive, too personal or jewelry. What does she like? Certain sports or music? Plays?"

"Yeah, all of that, but nothing specific. Unless I haven't picked up on that kind of thing." He stopped himself, thinking. "Antiques. At least she likes to go looking for them. She never buys anything." He shot me a terrified look. "You're not saying I need to buy something she's admired when I've gone with her?"

"No. But maybe you could do something personal around that theme?"

"Like what?"

"Aren't there some small towns around here that are known as great places to look for antiques?"

"Yeah, I think she's been to most of them already. It feels like she's dragged me to most of them, too, although I've only actually accompanied her to a few."

"Dragged, huh? Does she realize that's how you feel about the experience?"

"No. Well, okay, I joke about it occasionally. A lot. Antiques don't do anything for me, Ro. I hope you're not suggesting I develop a sudden interest in teapots and figurines."

"The Luann I know wouldn't want you to pretend something you don't feel. But she would like it a lot if you acknowledged you know how she feels."

"You're trying to lead this old horse to a stream of water apparently you see, but I don't. Yet."

"You're getting there, though. Give it a shot."

"That's it? You're done helping?" He sounded like a petulant kid being told he had to finish his homework on his own.

"For now. Besides, we need to find Muriel Fox while what we learned from Karl Backstrom is still fresh in our brains."

His issue about the perfect gift for Luann must really be bothering him, or he would've been champing at the bit to interview the woman. Of course, Christmas was now not much more than a week away. If it were me, I would've made a decision like that weeks ago and have the gift wrapped and hidden away by now. No, wait. That wasn't me. With Mehaffy House and the Rendezvous so much on my mind for the past month, I'd taken care of a gift for Chuck some time ago and hadn't given the subject much thought since.

Why was that?

Who was I fooling? I tended to suppress anything personal about Chuck while I was still figuring out what I wanted our future to be. Chuck appeared to know. He kept almost bringing up the serious discussion we needed to have, and I kept putting him off.

Why?

I loved the man. I'd already crossed that bridge. But Chuck wanted more. A lifetime commitment. Maybe not the formality of marriage, but something permanent. I did, too, but I'd been holding back for some reason. Ben? Was I afraid of losing another man in my life? Granted, it had been horrible to live through my husband's cancer and his death, but I'd come through that period. I'd survived the car crash that ended my field career as a homicide investigator and found a rich new career in home renovation. And learned to live my life on my own. Was that it? Was I hesitant to change that status? Or did I not want to?

I came out of my self-reflection to realize we were nearing Muriel Fox's home. I was anxious to go knock on her door and proceed with this investigation. Anything to keep me from answering those last two questions.

CHAPTER 9

uriel Fox's house was located in the part of town where older trees provided a shady canopy for the inhabitants and protection from the sun, whose rays, even though it was December, were still quite warm. Unfortunately, the house itself received little of that shelter. Though not peeling, the once white paint had yellowed.

"Come in," she said after we'd rung the bell. "I've been expecting someone official to show up to tell me about the accident, since I guess I'm the one in charge of the business now." Appearing to be in her mid-forties, she reminded me of the nursing assistants who did the initial intake procedures during my annual physicals: efficient, focused on what they had to do, unsmiling.

"We can't say officially yet," Herc told her, taking a seat in her small but tidy living room. I followed suit in another chair while Muriel Fox took a place in the middle of a small sofa. He introduced me and proceeded with our interview. "What we can say from an official perspective is that it wasn't an accident. Your boss, Terry Seiser, was killed."

She sat forward. "Killed? You mean someone intentionally caused that viewing stand to collapse?"

"That's the way it appears. We were told you'd been there," Herc continued.

She nodded. "Yes. I wasn't there to assist him. He'd made it quite clear he didn't need any help. But he couldn't keep me away from the race itself. He'd approved my day off long ago, before he ever got involved in the event. He tried to counteract his approval, but I convinced him there'd be little foot traffic at the hardware store while the marathon was on. The part-time help could handle whoever showed up."

"Were you entered in the race?" I asked.

"No. I wanted to be there to root on friends who were running. I don't know much about marathons, so I went early to get a good position from which to see them go by. I chose a spot near the starting line where they could see me right off, so I didn't hear about the accident, uh, collapse of the stand, until I heard about it from others. By the time I'd walked over to check it out, the EMTs were taking him away. Your people wouldn't tell me much when I asked what happened. I came home and waited to hear about it on the news."

"You didn't know your boss was the victim?" I asked.

"No, although I suspected as much given that it involved the viewing stand. The news people on the radio held up announcing the name of the victim until just a little while ago."

"We're sorry you had to learn about his death that way," I said. "Are you here by yourself?"

"Yes. I live alone. If you're worried about how I'm taking it, don't. I'm shocked, yes, but not in shock."

"What's your job at the hardware store?" Herc asked.

"My main responsibility is the accounting end of the business. I'm usually behind the scenes in the office. Terry handled most of the purchasing, although I took care of the smaller, regular inventory. He was also the customer relations part."

I'd gotten the impression from Karl that she did most of the work, but so far she was guarded in her response. "How long have you worked there?" I asked, hoping she'd shed more light on her role.

"About sixteen years. I got the job right after graduating from high school. Old Mr. Seiser was still in charge then."

"How did you get along with the victim?" Herc asked.

Her forehead wrinkled, like she hadn't fully understood his question. "Okay. We weren't close friends, but we'd worked together so long, we'd gotten used to each other's ways."

At least she hadn't claimed they were good friends, as so many close to the victim tended to do whether that had been the case or not.

"Did he share much about his marathon assignment with you?" I asked.

"No, very little. I didn't even know he was involved until this woman came in early last week to go over details with him. He told me to watch the store and closed the door to the office once they were inside. It was only as she was leaving that I got any inkling what was going on. 'Thanks again for all your help with the marathon, Terry,' she said. I guess he felt then he needed to share a little something, which was about all it was. He said he'd been asked by the community group putting on the race to put together a jazzy viewing platform from which the winners could be recognized."

"What was your reaction? Did your business typically participate in community events like the race?" I asked.

She stared at me like I'd asked a question in a foreign language. "No. Terry didn't have much of a life outside the hardware store and the lumberyard. Anything having to do with the community was way outside his usual activities."

Finally, we'd gotten a little more insight into the man's behavior. "How do you explain this unusual step?" I asked.

She blinked. "I can't. Like I said, he didn't share things like that with me."

"What about the woman who was working with him on the marathon? Was that the first time you'd seen her?"

"Yes, although since then I've seen her on local TV promoting the race. Her name is Ellen something."

"Ellen Garvey," Herc said. No need to hide what was already public knowledge. "Are you aware if she'd called him or got in touch with him otherwise?"

"No, although in recent weeks he'd hole up in his office, locking the door, more often than usual. He could have been talking to her then." She appeared to consider her reply. "I guess it sounds fishy that I didn't ask him more about her, but I'd learned long ago not to push for personal information. He was a private man. He'd either clam up or tell me it was none of my business."

"Was he like that around the store with business issues?" I asked.

"He was quick to let you know if you'd made a mistake, if that's what you mean."

"What about praising good work?" I pursued.

She snorted, although she quickly caught herself. "That wasn't his style."

"What's the story with the lumberyard?" Herc asked. "When you mention the business, you refer to the store. Are you including the lumberyard in that statement?"

"One of the last things old Mr. Seiser did before he passed was to buy the lumberyard next door when it came on the market with the understanding that the current staff remain. That was mainly the manager, the assistant manager and four staff. Since then, the manager retired, and the guy who'd been assistant manager, Gordo Zaharian, took over. Two of the staff have moved on, and they haven't been replaced."

"Are you saying the lumberyard has operated independently?" Herc asked.

"Up to a point. Old Mr. Seiser set up a corporate structure where the lumberyard manager technically reported to the head of the business, as well as profits from the lumberyard went into the corporate pot, but for all intents and purposes, the lumberyard was independent. Other than whenever Terry helped himself to its inventory."

"How has that worked?" I asked.

She bit a lip and briefly studied her nails. "Terry thought it was working well. You'd have to ask Gordo or anyone else at the lumberyard for their opinion."

In other words, relations between Seiser and Gordo Zaharian weren't good. We'd have to find out for ourselves later.

Time to follow up on her opening remark. "Your first words when we got here were that you guessed you were in charge of the business now. Please explain," I said.

She shrugged. "I spoke out of turn. Nerves, I guess. Terry has been divorced for years and had no children, although there is one cousin. I think there's a will because on occasion Terry has hinted I was named in it, but there is no succession plan for the business. His attorney is Joshua Collins, if you want to check with him."

"What are your current plans for the store?" I asked.

"After I heard about his death, I couldn't face going back in today. I called the kid who works there part-time and told him to place a sign on the door saying the place is closed until further notice due to a death. That he should lock up and go home. I'll go in tomorrow or Monday and try to put things in order."

"How would you describe the health of the business?" I asked.

"I'm not sure what you mean."

"You're the one who keeps the books, Ms. Fox," I told her. "If anyone knows if the place is doing booming business or barely surviving, that should be you."

She closed her eyes briefly. Once again, her nails received her attention. "We've been able to keep the doors open. In these strange economic times, that's saying a lot."

"Have you been in touch with Mr. Zaharian since you learned of Mr. Seiser's death?"

"He called me. I told him to hold tight as far as what would happen to the business was concerned. It was up to him if he wanted to close for the day or close indefinitely, like I planned to do with the hardware store."

Herc asked for Zaharian's contact information, which she readily supplied.

"Am I, uh, considered a suspect?" she asked after Herc handed her his card.

"We're just getting started, Ms. Fox. At this point, we have no reason to arrest you, but you appear to have been one of the few people close to the victim."

"That woman? Ellen Garvey, I think you called her. Is she a suspect?"

Herc went deeper into police mode. "Can't share any of that information. Why do you ask? Do you have some reason to think she'd want him dead?"

"Nothing specific. But there must've been something between them if he came out of his usual shell and agreed to take charge of that viewing stand."

"Anyone else we should talk to?" I asked.

"His housekeeper, Carmen Loomis. Besides me, she probably saw him most. I don't know her, just of her because she'd call him from time to time and I'd take the call." She gave us Seiser's home address and Loomis's phone number.

At the door, she had one more suggestion. "Talk to Gordo. Terry would have needed inventory from the lumberyard to build that platform. Gordo would know more about that."

As we left, I had this feeling of having finished half a meal. Muriel Fox wasn't exactly hostile, but she clearly hadn't provided as much information as she could have. Why? What was she keeping from us?

"Who do we talk to next? The housekeeper or the lumberyard manager?" Herc asked as we got in the car.

"The housekeeper should know more about the man himself. And my guess is that Gordo Zaharian will have a lot to tell us whenever we meet up with him."

"The housekeeper it is. What are your thoughts before we get there?"

"Muriel Fox did her best to answer our questions with as little personal opinion as possible. Something's going on there. We need to chip away at her reticence," I replied. "And that business? Even with as little as she told us, there's something definitely wrong there. We need to get hold of their books before the attorney prevents us."

"Same with the lumberyard," Herc said. "The way that working relationship has been structured, there's a bomb just waiting to explode. Maybe that's what happened this morning."

"Maybe. We'll get a better feel for the degree of dissention once we talk to Zaharian. I don't think we can dismiss Ellen Garvey either. Fox clearly didn't like her. Jealousy? I don't think so. I didn't pick up on any romantic vibes she felt for her boss, but then, she did a pretty good job of hiding her feelings overall."

Herc had another thought to share. "Surprised me that Seiser appears to have made no plans for succession. Especially since he didn't have any family to speak of."

"There's always Al," I said. "Do you think he'll wind up owning the business?"

He laughed. "Wouldn't that be a hoot? He begs you to step in for him investigating this murder and then he inherits the whole thing."

I turned to Herc. "You're kidding, right?"

"Only halfway, Ro. Not sure how I'd feel about it if that possibility came to pass."

CHAPTER 10

At Seiser's home, we found a small scrap of black fabric draped around the doorbell. I remembered my parents doing the same when my grandmother died, but I hadn't seen much of this tradition since then.

The door opened to reveal an upside-down triangle of a woman, dressed in black. Her most notable feature was her deep-set dark eyes, rimmed in red at the moment. Her hair reminded me of a clump of drying grass, and her sallow complexion may have never met a moisturizer.

"Yes?" she said.

Herc immediately identified us and requested entry. She identified herself as Mrs. Carmen Loomis. I recalled that Al had told us she was a widow he met on a case several years ago and had wound up recommending her to his cousin.

"Have you learned any more about Mr. Seiser's accident?"

"How did you hear?" he asked.

"On the TV. I don't usually watch much on Saturdays. I don't care for sports, and that's all that seems to be on. But something told me I should tune in today."

"What did the news report about the accident?" I asked.

"Not much. No one seemed to know what had happened

except some structure on the marathon route collapsed on top of him. They said Terry, Mr. Seiser, was dead on the scene, but no one who knew anything would say. They promised more details later."

"It has since been established that he was killed. Your boss was murdered," Herc told her. He was direct on purpose, to see how she'd react.

"Murdered? Mr. Seiser?" She shook her head repeatedly, her hand covering her mouth. "No, no, it can't be. He may have seemed unfriendly to some, but I can't believe that was reason enough to kill him."

"Then you got on well with him?" I asked, surprised someone may have actually liked the man.

"For the most part, yes. He depended on me to run this household properly."

"How long have you worked for him?"

"Fifteen years next March."

For such a disagreeable guy, this was the second woman who'd stuck by him for a long time. What was it about the man that elicited such loyalty? "Are you the only staff here?"

"Yes. I'm his housekeeper and cook. My living quarters are at the back of the house."

"Do you know anything about the project he was working on for the marathon?" I asked.

"The viewing stand? He left the plans out one night where anyone, me, could see them. He didn't tell me about it. That wasn't his way. But I could tell he was excited about it. His mood changed in the last few weeks."

"How?" Herc asked.

"Just little things. There was a bounce in his step. That kind of thing. He even complimented me on a meal one night."

"Mind if we look around?" Herc asked.

"Do you have a warrant?"

"No, but I can get one," he replied.

"I don't have a problem with you doing so, but let me check with his attorney first."

She excused herself to make the call.

"Looks like we'll be waiting on a warrant," Herc said out of her hearing.

But to our surprise, Joshua Collins, the attorney, said to go ahead with a search of the house, but if we planned to search the business, a warrant would be necessary. He advised Mrs. Loomis to do whatever we asked to assist in the investigation. I understood the requirement for the business; he was protecting the business entity. As for the residence, with Seiser gone, Collins apparently was more concerned in helping us find whatever we could to discover the murderer than protecting his client's privacy.

The small, two-story older home from the fifties had three bedrooms and a bath upstairs. The downstairs included the front living room, the combination kitchen-dining room, and a small room and bath in the back, where Mrs. Loomis lived.

We started upstairs with Seiser's bedroom. To characterize it as utilitarian would be an understatement. It was furnished with a double bed and a chest of drawers. The bed had been neatly made with a navy corded duvet. The chest held two half drawers on top and two full drawers on the bottom. The contents of the bottom two included two sets of pajamas and underwear, all folded and stacked or placed in order.

One of the two top half-drawers contained handkerchiefs, an old wallet, a pocket watch, a pair of cufflinks with the monogram EWS and dress socks. The other held a couple of document-size manila envelopes. The wallet was empty except for a card that said William Seiser and a telephone number. We photographed the card as well as the jewelry, which apparently had belonged to him. The stack of documents we bagged after filling out a receipt for Mrs. Loomis.

The second bedroom was smaller with only a bed with no

bedding, just a yellowed mattress atop it. The third had been serving as his office with a desk, chair, filing cabinet, old desktop computer and a printer. The filing cabinet contained too many documents for the two of us to catalog and take with us. "I'll have someone on the team come by her later today and box up the contents as well as the computer for us to review later," Herc said. The same applied to the contents of the desk. One drawer was locked, but we found the key in with the various pencils, pens and notepads.

"Does anything we've found suggest a motive for murder?" I asked. "So far, I'm drawing a blank."

"The same for me. Maybe we'll find something in the papers we found in his bedroom. We probably should take a gander at them while we're still here, in case we need to ask the house-keeper follow-up questions, but I want to get to that lumberyard guy yet today."

The bathroom revealed little of interest, unless parties unknown had poisoned his toothpaste, mouthwash or the bottle of painkillers. At this point, we had no reason to suspect that had happened, so we left them for now. One thing we did learn: he apparently had no prescription drugs, suggesting he was either in good shape or never saw a doctor.

Like the upstairs, the condition of the downstairs was immac-ulate. The living room was sparsely furnished, just a sofa, two easy chairs and a TV set. The kitchen showed no traces of any recent meals. No dirty dishes, not even in the dishwasher. Inside the fridge we found four bottles of beer, several pieces of fried chicken neatly packaged in a storage container and the usual assortment of condiments. The freezer was well stocked with wrapped packages of meat and frozen meals, all marked. On a recent case, we'd found an incriminating piece of evidence in the freezer. No such thing was apparent this time.

"It would appear Mrs. Loomis has been earning her money," I said, impressed with the woman's housekeeping skills. "She'll probably be out of a job now that Seiser is gone. Perhaps you should snatch her up before anyone else does."

"Are you implying I'm a slob?"

I couldn't tell if he was seriously insulted or giving me a hard time. "You rarely invite me to your place, but if the state of your car's interior is any indication, I'd say you might need help. Especially if Luann will be at your place on occasion. She hasn't been there yet, has she?"

"Well, no. We've either gone out or to her place, which isn't exactly the epitome of clean, if you want to know. But me hire a housekeeper? I can't afford that."

"Okay. Just sayin'."

We moved on to what must've been Loomis's room, but not until after we'd dealt with her objections.

"That bedroom and the attached bath are my private quarters," she said.

"They're still part of the victim's personal domain," Herc replied, refusing to back down.

"What do you hope to find there?" she asked, not ready yet to concede.

"We have no idea, Mrs. Loomis. We're attempting to discover anything we can about who would want your boss dead."

"Surely you don't think I killed him?"

"We're not accusing you of anything. For now."

"Terry, Mr. Seiser, gave me this job when no one else seemed interested in helping a recent widow get back on her feet. Why would I repay him like that?"

Herc didn't reply. Instead, he invited her to stand in the entrance to her room to observe while we searched. She took him up on his offer.

Her bedroom included a few more creature comforts than her boss's room. A medium-size flat-screen TV took up space on one wall. A comfy chintz easy chair occupied one corner, and a recliner resided in the other. Nothing was out of order. Her small bathroom was spotless. Her medicine cabinet contained mouthwash, toothpaste, one vial of mild tranquilizers and several bottles, tubes and jars of moisturizers and other beauty creams, which was a surprise to me. Though the top of the vanity only held a magnifying mirror and a water glass, the drawer underneath was a hodgepodge of lipsticks, face powder, mascara, eye shadow containers and eyeliners. Not unusual, except the woman who stood watching us from the doorway wore no makeup.

"Do you own a computer of any type, Mrs. Loomis?" I asked.

"I might. Do you have the authority to search it too?"

"I'm only asking. Our field team will be here later to pick up Mr. Seiser's computer. It's part of the contents of the house." I looked to Herc to follow up.

He picked up my cue. "Your computer, if you do have one, is your property. We'll respect that. For now. Like we said when we first arrived, we're here to obtain whatever information we can from you about your employer."

She bit a lip and briefly clutched her hands. "I'm sorry. Mr. Seiser didn't have many visitors here at the house. I guess I'm not used to being around other people, other than him. I'm especially not used to dealing with the police."

She'd left herself open. I had to pursue her statement. "Why is that, Mrs. Loomis? If we checked, would we find you have a criminal record?"

She let down her guard enough to enter the room a few feet. "No, that's not the case. The only person in law enforcement I know is Aloysius Buford. Long ago, just after my husband died from injuries suffered in a work accident, I was the victim of a robbery. I'd pretty much emptied our bank account and mortgaged our house to the hilt for my husband's care, so when someone broke into the house while I still lived there and took everything else of value, I was destitute and believed I'd soon find myself out on the street. Officer Buford couldn't find the culprit, but he did set me up with his cousin, Terry Seiser."

That explained why she agreed to cook and clean for Mr. Personality. Probably no one else would. But that was years ago. Why hadn't she looked for a more agreeable employer over the years? "From what I've seen about the way you keep this house,

I'm surprised someone else hasn't stolen you away at some point over the years."

Her face colored slightly. "Uh, yes. Someone tried once or twice."

I might be getting off track, but I wanted to know more about this woman. "If you'll excuse my asking, why didn't you accept?"

"I considered one, but in the end decided Mr. Seiser needed me more."

That spoke volumes. Something to file away, but I decided not to pursue it more now. If Herc picked up on her feelings, he didn't explore them further either. He always tended to take his leads from me in what he liked to call "touchy-feely" situations.

Herc handed her the receipt for the documents we were taking with us that had come from the drawer in Seiser's bedroom. "That's all we need for now, Mrs. Loomis," he told her. "If you think of anything else that might be helpful, please give me a call."

CHAPTER 11

couldn't wait to get to the car to start flipping through the stack of documents. Maybe they would finally help us make some sense of the man's death.

"Before I lose you to that pile of info you're so anxious to get to, gimme your first impressions of that woman," Herc said as he started the car.

"She keeps a very clean house, like I told you before."

"I hear your not-so-subtle hint. What else?"

I didn't have to think about my response. Two notions had been running through my head. "She cared for him, more than she wanted to let on. And though she appeared to us as a plain, middle-aged woman, she has the capability to glam up."

"You got all that just from talking to her and going through the house?"

"She's done a bang-up job of cleaning Seiser's house. Skills like that are becoming more and more difficult to find, so why was she still working for him after so many years? She said she'd been approached by other employers more than once, but she'd turned down those jobs. Why? My guess is that was more than loyalty. She had a thing for him. Whether he was aware of it or not we still need to discover."

"You got all that just from the fact she's worked so long for the guy?" Herc asked.

"You only saw the cooler version of Terry Seiser last night," I replied. "I tangled with the real guy when I asked him to donate a few items to the Rendezvous. The term *jerk* doesn't go far enough to describe the man's persona, but it's the best I can think of now. I can't believe anyone would stay with him so many years unless he was paying her a fortune or …"

"Or she was in love with him?" He didn't sound convinced.

"Then there was the stash of makeup we found in her vanity drawer. It didn't occur to me at the time to open any of them to see if they'd been used. If we need to talk to her again, especially with the aid of a warrant, it should include that option."

He didn't speak for a couple beats. Then he attempted to expand on my comment about the makeup. "Like, did she buy them with dreams of transforming herself, or were they used at some point? If they were, when and why? And why wasn't she wearing any makeup today? Not even lipstick. Not wearing makeup tells you something about her personality. Maybe she doesn't use it when she's cleaning? Or maybe she anticipated our visit and dressed to impress us. Maybe she's actually a hottie, but she didn't want us to know."

"Good points, Herc. I'm not agreeing, but I'm not throwing them out either."

"Do you think she's a suspect?" he asked, moving on to the real question.

"I'm not ruling her out. No particular motive immediately springs to mind, but we're just getting started. Like I said, there's more to her than she's letting on, although that may have nothing to do with his murder."

"What are you finding in those papers?"

"A bunch of stuff related to the marathon." I quickly flicked through the pile of papers. "Newspaper clippings from the time it was first announced until the most recent article yesterday.

There's also some stuff copied from the internet about marathons and a few articles about Ellen Garvey."

Herc screwed up his face, apparently absorbing my comments. "Interesting. That stuff doesn't tell us whether the idea of constructing the viewing stand was his or Ellen Garvey's, but the idea was on his radar screen at least since that first article on the marathon appeared."

"Also interesting that it was in his bedroom drawer rather than his home office," I said.

"Hiding it from his housekeeper?"

I couldn't help but laugh. Okay, snort. "Herc, believe me, Carmen Loomis knows every inch of that house. If he wanted to hide anything from her, he'd leave it at the hardware store."

"Then that office manager would've found it," he said.

"Most likely, now that you've pointed that out, unless there's someplace at the store she's not allowed to see."

"Like the men's room?" he threw out.

"Even from what little we learned from her so far, I doubt she would've avoided the men's room, if it suited her purposes to go in there."

"Where else, then?"

"I don't know right now. We definitely have to revisit his place of business as well as talk to Muriel Fox again. Soon, before she gets rid of anything incriminating," I said.

"You think she's our killer?"

"Too soon. You know that, Herc. I just got strange vibes from her, along the same line as those I received from Loomis. Same but different."

"Both ladies are on my suspect list, but my vibe receptors aren't as acute as yours. Explain what you mean."

"Both have been with him for years. That would've taken a special kind of endurance. Loyalty, perhaps. I already said I think the Loomis woman has/had a thing for him. Maybe it was the same for Muriel Fox. We need to spend more time with her and gather more information."

About that time, I glanced up from the papers I'd been surveying. "Is this the direction to Gordo Zaharian's house?" I asked Herc.

"Thought we should go to the station and give that stack of documents a closer look before we track down Zaharian."

Although I'd pretty much taken in what there was to see in the stack I'd been perusing, Herc deserved his chance to make what he could of them.

At his suggestion, I updated his research assistant, Janet Oliver, on the case once we got to the station. In the old days, Herc and I spent much more time in the office tracking down information about suspects. That was in the days before computers got so sophisticated. Nowadays, not only did they do much more of the legwork for us, Herc had Janet using those computers much more expertly than the two of us. She'd been a great support in the more recent cases in which I'd participated. One of these days, probably sooner than Herc and I were ready, she'd move on, either to higher administrative positions within the department or she'd decide she was ready to become a cop.

"I'm not a runner," Janet said, "but I went to the park to see Isla and Greg race." Isla Dexter and Greg Ennis were two rookie cops who worked with Herc from time to time. The three of them had become quite close. "I got there just as the ambulance was pulling away."

"It's your day off. Why are you here?"

She chuckled knowingly. "Sixth sense. Although the news called it an accident, I saw you and Lieutenant Morgan talking excitedly with Sergeant Buford near the accident site. I'd been off in another part of the park to see the start of the race when I heard there'd been an incident near the finish line. I couldn't get any closer, but it didn't take much for me to guess there was more involved than an accident. I thought you might need me, so I came into the office and got started doing some background work."

I sat back and took in this miracle of police investigative

science. "Don't ever doubt that sixth sense. It will take you far in this line of work. What have you found thus far?"

"The victim, Mr. Seiser, has had a few minor skirmishes in the past in which law enforcement had to intervene, but he wasn't charged. He has been the owner and manager of Seiser's Hardware and Lumberyard for seventeen years, inheriting it from his father, William Seiser. In the year before William Seiser's death, William purchased Shasta Lumber and legally put it under the umbrella of his hardware concern."

Most of this Herc and I had already gleaned from Fox and Loomis, but Janet's research verified it and gave us a base from which to build a picture of the guy. "How about financials? Have you gotten that far?" I asked her.

Her forehead wrinkled. "I started but ran into a roadblock of sorts. On the surface, both the hardware store and the lumberyard are still bringing in revenue, the lumberyard more than the store. But it seems to disappear into a sort of black hole after being deposited. Then new figures emerge. They don't match the earlier amount but they're not far off. I wish Sergeant Buford was here. Now that he's become a specialist in police forensic accounting, he might be able to track the money trail better."

"Don't dismiss your capabilities, Janet." On occasion, I'd noticed she would sometimes put herself down. She'd never get anywhere in police work if she didn't get past that tendency. "For as little time as you've had to get into the man's story this morning, you've made significant progress. If you had trouble following the money, then maybe there's a reason."

"Like what?" she asked.

"I don't know. From my limited dealings with the man, I wouldn't be surprised if he was doing business under the counter or even embezzling from his own business."

"Or perhaps he's not the same businessman his father was," she said.

I considered that theory. "Somehow he's managed to keep the store going for years. Maybe his father had established such a good rep, he's been living on that all this time, but little by little that patina has been slipping away."

"I guess that's possible."

"We've already spoken with the woman who's been his business manager and bookkeeper. We plan to resume that interview on Monday when she's recovered from her shock. Now we have more reason than ever to talk with her." My brain got ahead of me, thinking of how that discussion might go. "We'll need some specific questions to ask her to gauge the health of the business. Could you put those together for us?" She wasn't my staff person to ask to do such work, but both she and Herc would be okay with my doing so.

"Of course, although both you and the lieutenant are sharper where it concerns finances than you give yourselves credit for."

"What makes a guy who's spent most of his life being antisocial suddenly take on such a major community-oriented project?" Herc asked rhetorically as he joined us in this discussion, having glanced through the documents we brought back with us.

"Apparently that stash from his bedroom drawer didn't provide any clues?" I said.

"Not the reason why he was collecting data on marathons. What we really need is the transcript from his emails, phone calls and texts, since his phone is no longer workable. Who has he been talking to recently? What did he ask? What did they tell him?"

"I'll check on that now, Lieutenant. Can't promise much yet. It's a smaller staff than usual today as so many took the day off for the marathon," Janet replied.

I asked Janet to brief him about her findings regarding Seiser's finances. "How about his own personal finances?" he asked after she finished.

"I couldn't find much," she said. "Under a thousand dollars in his bank account. Minor stock holdings. His only property, his home and a ten-year-old pickup. And the store and lumberyard."

"Maybe that accounts for his emergence into community activities," I said. "He was seeking to increase his revenue by raising his public image. That's a long-term plan, though, and if he needed more immediate financing, it wouldn't pay off soon enough."

Herc shook his head. "I don't know, Ro. This guy was looking for something much more immediate. I don't know how I know; I feel it in my blood. Your touchy-feely approach to investigation has finally gotten to me."

"Don't discount that feeling, Herc. You're so devoted to going by the evidence, maybe it's there and we just don't realize it yet."

He blew out a breath. "If that's the case, what is it?"

"Too soon, my friend. We just got started on this a few hours ago. We made good progress. We have a plan for who to talk to next. And our good friend here has begun collecting a very solid database."

"Yeah," he replied grumpily. "I know all that. I'm frustrated because his actions aren't making any sense."

"Maybe you need a break?" Janet said.

"So soon?" he replied.

"Lunch. That's what I meant," she said. "Why don't you two treat yourselves to some carbolicious fast food for an hour or so and then resume your interviews?"

"Carbolicious?" I said. "Even if such a word doesn't exist, I like the way you think, Janet. Want to go with us?"

"Thanks, but I'm watching the carbs myself right now. Isla and Greg gave me a tough time about not participating in the race with them. I've been thinking maybe I should put myself on a fitness routine, especially if I plan to enter the Academy at some point."

"Academy?" Herc shrieked. "Oliver, please tell me you're not gonna become a cop."

"I've been thinking more and more about it, Lieutenant, but I haven't made up my mind."

He blew out another breath. "You'd make a great cop, Janet. I don't want to stop you. It's just that …"

"We both appreciate all you do for us now as a researcher," I said before he started blubbering.

She pulled one of her errant blond curls behind her ear. "Thank you. Don't get me wrong. I've had the time of my life working with the two of you during the last few months. You've made me feel like an integral part of the team. It's just that ..."

"You want to be in on the action," I supplied for her.

She offered a shy smile but didn't reply.

"Yeah, we get it," Herc said, his tone somewhere between begrudging and accepting. "We were both there when we were young pups in the department a million years ago. There's a high like nothing else when you uphold public safety by catching the bad guys, even with considerable danger to yourself. Just ..."

"Don't rush into my decision until I've truly thought how it can change my life," she said.

"We're both here for you if you have any questions about taking the plunge," I told her.

"Thanks, you guys. I'll keep that in mind. I've already told my mom when she's worried about my working for the police that I've got the greatest of mentors looking out for me."

CHAPTER 12

"How 'bout we put off lunch a little longer?" Herc said once we were on our way out of the building. "I know Janet suggested we needed our carbs, but I want to talk to that lumberyard guy before he's had any more time to revise his story about his dealings with Seiser."

"Who are you? Where's my partner, Hercules Morgan?"

"I know. I'd just like to move through this first day of investigating quicker than usual. It's a Saturday just before Christmas, and I've got personal matters to attend to. I've skipped enough holidays over the years paying attention to this job. We've gotta talk to this Zaharian guy and probably Ellen Garvey as well yet today. The rest can wait until Monday."

He hadn't come right out and said it, although if I'd let him talk longer, he might've declared how much he wanted to be spending time this evening with Luann.

My mouth gaped open as we pulled up to the address we'd been given for Gordo Zaharian.

"What's the matter?" Herc asked.

"It's an apartment building. An old one at that," I said. "I assumed a guy in charge of a lumberyard would live in a house, one he'd either built or restored."

"He's the manager, not the owner," Herc reminded me. "Apparently you've never done business with him?"

"No. I've left that part of our materials acquisition up to Val and Ryder. I'll ask them later what they know about him."

Gordo Zaharian reminded me of the warthog character in that animated film I'd seen years ago with Val. She loved the music and was convinced I'd like it too. And I had. Along with the charming story. Anyway, he was about five-nine with a receding hairline and shoulder-length medium-brown hair going gray. Although his shape reminded me of the warthog—large head, broad shoulders and burly body—that head of hair reminded me of a shaggy dog, that kind with hair that covered his eyes. He had a mustache and beard, also brown going gray.

"Any more news on Seiser?" he asked after Herc introduced us.

"His death has been determined to be a homicide," Herc said.

Zaharian jerked his head to the side. "It wasn't an accident? That's what Muriel Fox told me when she called and said to close the lumberyard for the day." He blew out a huff. "Like she was now in charge. We'll just see about that on Monday."

"But you did shut down for the day, correct?" Herc asked.

"Figured business would only be gossip hounds, not real customers. Thought I'd use the weekend to consider my options with him now out of the picture."

"Options?" I asked. Did he think just because Seiser was dead, the lumberyard was now an independent entity?

"Staying on and reporting to whoever takes over or finding another job. Neither appeals. If that Fox dame thinks she can just take over the reins, she's deluding herself. There's no way Seiser would've bequeathed it to her. She may picture herself as his faithful servant, but he's just been using her so-called talents all these years."

"And you know this how?" Herc asked.

"He didn't come over to the lumberyard much, just when he needed something, money, or wanted to remind me who was boss. But on a few occasions, he remained long enough to partake of our coffee and while there complained about running the hardware store, or more like having to deal with the ever-present Muriel Fox, who was constantly chiding him about something or other. He said his mother ran out on his dad and him years ago and there was no way he needed another woman like her in his life."

Interesting observation about Fox. Just the kind of thing we'd come for.

"Why doesn't your other option, leaving, appeal to you?" Herc asked.

"Look at me, man. I'm nearing fifty and not in the greatest shape. I had one year of community college when people were still using rotary phones. I got the job at the lumberyard when Seiser's old man bought the place and promised the previous owner he'd keep on all the staff."

"Who all does that include these days?" I asked.

"Me and Pauley Ventana. He was just a kid outta high school when we got bought. He's stayed with me ever since. Like me, he doesn't have a handful of skills going for him, but he's a good worker. Shows up on time and puts in a full day. About all I can ask."

"There's just the two of you?" Herc asked.

"Just the two of us remain from those early days, yeah. Lost the other two over the years, one who moved out of town shortly after the lumberyard was absorbed by the older Seiser, and the other retired about five years ago. The younger Seiser never approved replacing them on a full-time basis, but I could bring in part-time people when I begged enough. The last time he approved even part-time workers was two years ago."

"How do you explain that?" I asked.

He shrugged. "Did you ever meet the guy? I'll refrain from calling him the name I really want to use. Let's just say he wasn't a nice guy."

"That the only reason?" Herc asked.

"Money. At least that was always his excuse. Couldn't afford more staffing at this or that time of year. Never the right time."

"How did you deal with it, having only one other person working for you?" I asked.

He stared me down. "You look pretty bright to me, Mrs. Summerfield. With only two sets of hands, we could only do so much. We cut back where warranted and otherwise just got by. You figure it out."

"In other words, the lumberyard is suffering financially?" I said.

"We aren't going under. At least not yet. But we haven't been the cash cow the older Seiser saw in us for some time."

"If Seiser had approved adding more staff, would that have turned things around?" Herc asked.

Zaharian folded his arms in front of him. "I think so, although we'll never know, will we?"

"We'll want to see your books," Herc told him.

"Yeah, sure. But the books I keep are just the front end. I've had to report everything to Fox. I keep an honest set of books, which means I've found ways to incorporate the materials and cash he took from time to time. No way did I plan to set myself up for charges of fraud and embezzlement should he ever decide to come at me."

"We'll send someone by to get them on Monday," Herc said. "In the meantime, don't touch them or let anyone else touch them. Is that clear?"

"Okay. I get it. Are we done now?"

Since I'd been letting Herc do most of the talking, I took it from there. "One more question. Do you know anyone who disliked him so much they would've killed him?"

He didn't answer immediately. "Like I said before, he wasn't a nice guy. It's not so much that he made a lot of enemies. He just didn't have many friends. None I can think of now. Am I a suspect?"

I waited for Herc to answer. "You're one of the few people

who saw him frequently. You've already admitted you didn't like him."

"Along with most people," Zaharian replied. "I don't benefit from his death. In fact, as I've already pointed out, now that he's gone, I'm at loose ends. The only thing I gain from his death is not having to look at that sourpuss anymore."

Closing with the usual request to let us know if he thought of anything more that might help us with the case, we left.

"The guy doesn't mince words," I said once out of earshot.

"Or so he'd like us to believe. That business about not having any options now that Seiser is gone could be a cover. For all we know, he could be in cahoots with Muriel Fox so the two of them can take over the business."

Interesting theory. It hadn't occurred to me yet. "Could they do that legally?" I asked.

"At the moment, I have no idea. We'll need some legal consultation, if it comes to that. More reason to talk to that lawyer, Joshua Collins."

"I thought you wanted to call it a day soon?" I asked.

"I still do. I'll call Collins and make an appointment for early Monday morning, but I still want to catch Ellen Garvey yet today."

CHAPTER 13

"Do we really have to get into this now?" Ellen Garvey said after coming to her front door. "It's been a rough day. I already spoke to the officers on the scene."

"That was when everyone thought it was an accident," Herc said. "We've since determined it was murder."

Her hand shot to her mouth. "M-murder?" she managed to get out once she removed her hand. "How? I mean what makes you think that? The viewing stand fell on him and, uh, crushed him to death."

Herc nodded as we let ourselves into the well-appointed but modest living room of her home. "That's true. But first he was hit on the head and lugged unconscious under the stand before it collapsed."

She shook her head vehemently. "No! That's horrible. How could someone do such a thing?" Tears came to her eyes.

"That's what we're trying to find out, Ellen," I said. "And why we're here now while the incident is still fresh in everyone's mind. You were there. Maybe not on the scene but somewhere in the park. We need to hear your impressions before they start to blur over the next few days. That's a normal reaction when someone tries to make sense of something that is senseless."

"Yes, I was in the park, but like you just said, I was nowhere near the viewing stand."

Herc consulted his notebook computer. "The notes from the first officers on the scene say that you showed up in a golf cart shortly after they arrived."

"Yes, that's true. One of the park employees was talking to the investigating officers when I got there. I guess that's who found him, or rather, the wreckage, and he called the police. No one knew Terry was under it until I asked about his whereabouts. The realization he must have been under it hit us all about the same time."

She closed her eyes as if attempting to turn off the scene in her mind and fell into the nearest chair.

"You're still in shock about what you witnessed," I said gently, "but please stay with us a little longer. Someone caused that platform to fall. That kind of decision didn't occur on the spot. It was planned and deliberate. It's up to us to figure out who and why."

She reached for a nearby box of tissues and dabbed at her eyes. "You're right. I'll try to help you. What do you want to know?"

"Is a viewing stand like the one Mr. Seiser constructed a typical element in marathons like the Reindeer Run?" Herc asked.

"I'm the wrong person to answer that question. I'm not a runner and before this event didn't know anyone who was."

"How did you get involved with this race then?" I asked.

She let her shoulders fall, more at ease with this question. "That's rather complicated. My late husband was an early pioneer in transitioning old-time filling stations to the more modern model of the convenience store. When he died five years ago, he left me a very wealthy widow. I had more money than I knew what to do with and had relatives, friends and strangers coming at me night and day asking for donations for a variety of causes, some of them legit but more just scams. The only way to survive was to find a financial advisor I trusted who wouldn't take advantage of me."

"Given your current reputation," I said, "you must've found that person."

"I had to fire the first two. Their hearts were in the right place, but their knowledge of finance was minimal. Anyway, I finally found Martin Brockhurst three years ago. He started me out small as a contributor to a few causes but not the driving force behind them. Since my late husband, Neils, was born and raised in this part of the state and he made his fortune throughout Florida, I decided to limit my financial support to local and area causes."

"We know most of that from the press releases that accompanied the Run, but how did you get hooked up with this particular event?" I asked.

"Right. I wanted you to be aware of some of the background of my fundraising before I got to the Reindeer Run. I said I'm not a runner, but I do bike. I try to get out at least once weekly. When I was out one day last summer, I snapped the rim of my bike and wound up walking it and myself home. I flagged down the first car going my direction. I wouldn't normally accept rides from strangers, but I was winded and still a few miles from home. That driver turned out to be Carol McGiver, the executive director of Project Phoenix, the organization that supports low-income residences, most of which are in the older part of town thus far.

"Before you think it was a setup, just one more person with a cause manufacturing a reason to meet me, keep in mind there was no way she or I knew my bike would go wonkers at that very time and that she would show up right after to rescue me. On the way back to my place, we got to talking. When I asked her how she'd gotten involved with matching up lower income families with homes they could afford, she told me how years before she'd found herself in a similar situation. She'd been a teenager at the time her mother's home was condemned and then was swallowed up to become part of a new building project, one of my husband's stores.

"Although her mother was reimbursed the value of her home, for the next few years they struggled to find adequate housing they could afford. Those years left a major impression on her, something she vowed to address someday after she finished college."

"You wrote her a check then and there?" Herc asked, trying to nudge her toward the bottom line.

"No. It didn't happen like that. I did invite her in for a drink, though, when she dropped me off. Just as a courtesy. She turned me down because she was on her way to a meeting, so I offered to treat her to dinner afterwards. She asked if I'd meet her where she was speaking since she didn't know how long the meeting would last. As it turned out, she was just wrapping up her comments and answering audience questions when I arrived. I was about to return to the entrance when the gist of her responses sunk in. I found a seat near the back of the hall and within minutes was engrossed in the need for low-income housing in the area.

"If that was a setup, it was an elaborate one. But so be it. I got hooked. The idea for the marathon didn't come up for a few more weeks. We wanted to do something near the end of the year to coincide with both the holidays and end-of-the-fiscal-year charitable giving and also celebrate Florida's lovely weather this time of year. Martin Brockhurst, my financial advisor, suggested a marathon. Well, not technically a marathon. Those are 26.2 miles. We wanted something much shorter this first time. We decided on a 5K run, which is 3.1 miles. Martin's not a runner, but his brother, Wally, is.

"It was just one of many ideas we kicked around, but it appealed to me. It didn't relate directly to low-income housing, but I liked the health and outdoor aspects. We were running out of time, so I made an executive decision to go with it.

"Wally Brockhurst served as our initial technical advisor until details got more complicated and we had to find an actual marathon consultant. That turned out to be Cyrus Milligan."

"How did Terry Seiser get involved?" I asked, attempting to get us back to the subject at hand.

She continued to take her time answering, first flicking imaginary flecks from her pants leg and then rubbing her chin. "I know that's what you're here about, and I've been trying to get my thoughts about him in order ever since this morning. My relationship with him isn't easy to explain."

"How about we ask a few questions?" Herc said, trying to pin her down to something specific, although our questioning thus far had netted us this roundabout approach.

"All right," she replied.

After suggesting that approach, Herc glanced at me. *Thanks, guy.* "Let's start with the easy stuff," I said. "How long have you known him?"

"A few months. Shortly after Carol and I teamed up to raise funds for Project Phoenix, she asked me to accompany her on a few visits to local merchants to solicit both construction materials as well as contribute to our fundraising. Seiser's Hardware store was on the list."

This should be good. I'd been in a similar position just days ago. "And he turned you down flat," I said, getting ahead of her.

She cocked her head and stared at me like she couldn't believe my words. "Actually, no, although I got the impression he had been about to do that until he noticed me. Then he started to apologize, saying he wished he could, but it had been a tough couple of months for both the store and the lumberyard. We thanked him for his time and started to leave, and then he called out and asked us to hold on. He suggested we send him a list of the types of things we needed and he'd see if he had any inventory he could spare."

That didn't sound like the Seiser I knew. "Did he follow up? Donate some things?"

"Yes and no. A day or so after Carol emailed him the list, he called me. He'd, uh, asked for both our numbers when we first talked to him, but he only called me."

"You and not her?" Herc asked.

Her neck went pink. "Uh, yes. He said he thought he might

have some items for us but needed to clarify a few details first. Then he asked if we could discuss them over dinner that night."

Herc cleared his throat.

The woman hater apparently only despised certain women. Like me.

"I know, it was clearly a pickup line," Garvey said. "Better judgment told me to redirect his offer to Carol, but I, uh, didn't. I hadn't exactly lived a monk's life since Neils died, but I hadn't been seriously involved with anyone else either. Neils had been tall, athletic and good-looking. The men I'd seen since his death fit that pattern as well. Terry was, uh, just the opposite. He intrigued me. What I felt for him was something akin to what people who love horror films must experience. They know the end will be gory, but they can't look away. I saw a vulnerability in the very bark that turned others away."

Terry Seiser vulnerable?

"Go on," Herc said.

She stroked her neck. A stalling tactic or was it that difficult to admit she'd dated the man? "We started seeing each other socially after that. Others questioned what I saw in him, especially Carol, who'd been turned off by his rudeness from the beginning. I didn't try to defend his attitude. That would've been impossible. Instead, I simply suggested they'd get used to him in time.

"We were attending a cocktail party together along with a few other members of the marathon planning team when the idea of adding a viewing stand to the event arose. I'm not sure who mentioned it first, Terry or Cy, the consultant, but suddenly the concept took on a life of its own. Terry, who'd been hanging back and not saying much, got interested at that point.

"I forget whether Terry or Cy did the research. Apparently that type of apparatus isn't used all that often. At least for smaller events like ours. First one, then the other got excited at the prospect of doing something unique to enhance the marathon and attract more participants. Although Terry had initially suggested he could provide most of the materials free of charge, shortly after that, he said his office manager had cautioned him about giving away too much. The business couldn't absorb the cost. By then, Terry had officially joined the committee, and I'd named him the person in charge of the construction of the viewing stand."

Now we were getting somewhere. She finally didn't appear to be holding back. She was either still in shock or the significance of Seiser's role hadn't struck her yet.

"But since you went ahead with constructing the viewing stand, who underwrote the materials?" I asked.

"Cy and Carol and I batted that question around a bit before I offered to pay for everything against the funds we raised."

"How much did that amount to?" Herc asked.

"Carol and Muriel Fox, Terry's office manager, pointed out more than once it amounted to over ten thousand dollars. They wanted to be sure I was ready to underwrite that significant an amount."

"And you were?" Herc asked.

"I was good for the money, and at some point the idea arose that the platform could be broken down for use in future years for other events. That was an additional motivation. And by then I'd gotten excited about the feature myself."

"To clarify," I said, wanting to be sure we'd understood her correctly, "over ten thousand dollars was paid to Seiser's store?"

"Well, yes, I guess, although Terry was paid directly."

"Do you have a copy of the design plan?" Herc asked.

"No," she replied, waving off the question. "I approved the concept, the location and the expenditures, but I didn't get involved with the specific details like the design plan. Cy should have a copy."

"We'll talk to him, then," Herc said. "Do you have his contact information?"

"Yes. I'll jot that down, plus I'll give you the same for Carol McGiver and Martin Brockhurst."

"What plans did you have for security for the marathon?" Herc asked, thanks to what we'd learned from Henson.

"Security? The standard stuff, I guess, for an outdoors event in the park. Parking and crowd control. You need to talk to Cy about those specifics too. I think he was working with the park people on it."

Before we left her, I had one more question.

"Were you intimate with Terry Seiser?"

Once again, her hand came to her mouth. "That's my business."

"We'll respect your privacy, for now," I said. "But we can't guarantee we won't ask again if your answer becomes imperative to solving the case."

"Uh, okay. I'll keep that in mind."

CHAPTER 14

"Ellen Garvey doesn't live like a woman who inherited millions," I said to Herc as we walked to his car. "Although her dress last night screamed high price tag, today she's in a sweatshirt and jeans and lives in a nice but modest home."

"That's your take on all we just learned?" he replied.

"Safest comment before we're in your car."

He didn't reply until we both climbed inside. "Okay, spill. What did you get out of all that?"

"Why don't you go first for once?" I was just hassling him. He was anxious to call it a day and get on with whatever plans he had with Luann.

"Some holiday mood you're in. Okay, she had something going with Seiser. The mere fact she didn't want to answer your question about going to bed with him says as much."

"One more woman who wasn't turned off by the guy. What was it Shane said? Look for a woman behind his murder. Looks like we add Ellen Garvey to the list," I said.

"Motive?"

"Money," I replied. "Maybe she discovered the ten thousand

she'd okayed for the purchase of materials for the platform was going into his pockets instead repaying his business?"

"If that was the case, she was certainly playing dumb about the money part."

"Yeah, that's what struck me the most about the whole interview. She appeared to be up front with us and answered all our questions, even about the money. At no time did she say anything disparaging about him like a woman scorned."

"She did say he wasn't much to look at," Herc said.

"Minor point," I returned.

"So, her relationship with Seiser becomes point number one on our list. What else did you get?"

"Her explanation of how she came to be fundraising and especially fundraising for low-income housing went on forever. What do you make of that?"

Although he'd pulled away from her house, he only drove a block or two before parking to continue this discussion. He didn't want to go back to the station at the risk of getting more tied up there.

"Stalling? Hoping we'd not go near her relationship with Seiser?" I asked.

"That's one possibility. She could be totally legit and wanting to assist us with the case by giving us her background," he replied.

"Whether she meant to or not, she gave us two more persons of interest to talk to on Monday, Carol McGiver and Cyrus Milligan. Maybe even her financial advisor, Martin Brockhurst."

He scrunched up his forehead. "You don't think any of them killed Seiser, do you?"

I considered. "Probably not, although she didn't tell us much about Seiser's interactions with those folks. Still, given our questions about Ellen Garvey's veracity, their input could give us a better idea of who she is."

He fidgeted in his seat. "That it?"

"We also need that design plan from the Milligan guy. We still don't know how that platform could implode like it did. I want to see the schematics."

"Listen to you. One would think you know something about construction."

"Chuck? I'm home," I called as I entered our duplex. I'd started calling it "our" recently when he moved in. I figured if I said that enough around him, he'd be okay with continuing to live here rather than press for the three of us to move into his house. Or find a new one.

He didn't appear as quickly as he usually did when he was downstairs.

"Chuck? Your car's here, so you must be around somewhere."

Two seconds later, he sauntered into the kitchen wearing a very suspicious expression. A guilty expression. "Hi. You're home earlier than I anticipated. Are you done for the day?"

"Sure am! I'm yours until Monday morning."

"Barring some unforeseen wrinkle in the case," he said.

"Well, yes. But for now, let's enjoy the rest of the weekend. Unless you're involved with something else? Where were you anyway when I came in?"

"Me?" He made a show of rubbing his eyes. "You caught me. I was catching a short nap."

"Oh. A nap sounds like a good idea if you want me to join you?"

"Uh, sure, but I'm up now. Refreshed and ready for whatever you have in mind?" He raised a brow.

"Oh, okay. Do you still want to look for a tree?"

About that time, Jason wandered into the kitchen, red and green ribbons caught on his collar.

"Well, well. What have you been up to, my decorated friend?" I said to my feline greeter.

Chuck quickly dislodged the ribbons from Jason's collar. "You rat fink! You couldn't let me have just one little secret."

"Secret? Like in Christmas preparations?"

"Uh, yeah, something like that," he said. "I don't suppose you could forget what you just saw?"

"I doubt my cat will, but sure, I'll play along. Apparently the two of you have been up to activities you're not ready to discuss."

"Let's go find a tree. I know someone who owns a tree farm just outside of town."

"Of course, you do. You always *know someone.*"

"Just part of owning two eateries and a wine bar, Ro. I'm surprised you don't claim the same distinction as a cop."

"I'm not a cop. I'm a part-time consultant to the police department on homicide investigations," I replied a little too huffily. "And my contact with the public is from a totally different perspective than yours."

He raised both hands in surrender. "Okay, fine. I unwittingly touched a nerve. Mea culpa. Besides, as you so often point out, your real job these days is as part owner of Nailed It Home Renos. Change of subject—what kind of tree would you prefer?"

"Artificial. Less messy."

"Come on, Ro. It's our first Christmas together. Surely you want to mark this occasion with a bit more celebration?"

I touched his forearm. "Sure. I didn't realize a real tree was part of that." I should have. My mind had obviously not been tracking the same direction as his. *Get on board, Ro.* "Spruce. Blue spruce. Do you like those?"

He pulled me into his arms. "That's my girl. Woman. Good save."

I wasn't sure if the "save" part was my choice of blue spruce or his switch to the word woman. No point finding out. The day was still young enough, and it was time for me to put on my Santa hat.

The Christmas tree farm was five miles west of town, far enough out that even the newer housing developments faded into the background. I settled my shoulders against the luxurious seat back of Chuck's car and put the other events of the day behind me as I watched the still verdant fields and occasional stands of trees roll by.

I was expecting Santa and his elves to be on duty. Instead, a statuesque blonde walked up to the car. "You showed up just in time, Dawson. This year's inventory is quickly vanishing."

"Didn't want to pick something out without the input of my lady here. This is Rowena Summerfield, Britney. Ro, meet Britney Kellogg, Christmas tree entrepreneur extraordinaire."

She immediately stuck out her hand to me. "I'd heard you were off the market. Now I see why. I'm delighted to meet you, Rowena."

"Ro," I returned, sensing an immediate friend in the woman.

"And I'm Brit. What kind of tree are you thinking of today?"

"How's your stock of blue spruce?" Chuck asked. "Hope there's still a few good ones around."

"I think we can help you out there. How high?"

Chuck looked at me. "We haven't decided where to put it yet. What do you think about that front corner of the living room? The one farthest away from the door."

My designer instinct kicked in. Leave it to Chuck to do his part to bring me back to earth. "Great spot for it. Out of the way but still in a prominent place."

Brit personally led us off in one direction. Within twenty feet, I could see and smell the section reserved for the blue trees. "Are these what you had in mind?" I could hear the pride in her voice.

Chuck continued to hold my hand, but he pulled me forward like a kid being offered a lollipop. He didn't stop until we were almost standing inside the first tree in our path. Then he did drop my hand as he scuttled from tree to tree.

As far as I was concerned, any of these beauties would work just fine in my home, if they weren't too tall. I stood there and let him go through whatever mating dance this was with each delight of nature.

"Ro? Come over here," he called from somewhere inside the stand.

Brit, who'd remained behind with me, pointed to the left. "I think he's over there. C'mon. You may need a guide."

She was right. There was just enough room between trees for one human to pass, so I followed in her wake as best as I could. She was fast, and she knew where she was going. The last thing I wanted was to wind up lost in this sea of trees.

When I finally found them, Chuck was examining the tag attached to one tree. It had to be at least six and a half feet high. Could we even get it into our place?

"Well?" he said to me. "What do you think?"

"It's tall."

"Yeah, but it will fit," he replied.

"We could always shave an inch or two off the trunk," Brit said helpfully. "But I wouldn't recommend too much trimming. This is the height this tree was meant to be."

A purist. I couldn't blame her. These trees appeared to be more than product to her. They were her babies.

"I guess it would work. Though it'll take both of us to get it into the house. Do we even have a stand for it?"

"We have some here, if you don't," Britney said.

"Thanks, Brit. Yeah, we'll look at them. I've got an old one somewhere, but it's time to start fresh," Chuck said.

She called someone on her phone to come do the cutting while we headed off to pay for our purchase. Then a new thought occurred to me, and I pulled up. "Wait! I have a couple questions before you cut it down. I have a cat. A cat who's never been around a real tree. Will it be safe for him? It's not poisonous, is it? Sorry, I should've thought to ask sooner."

Brit offered a reassuring smile. "Not to worry, even if we had cut it down already. Blue spruce is nontoxic for children and pets, although the needles can get caught in the throat of an animal that gets too curious."

I blew out a relieved breath. I didn't want to spoil the holiday for Chuck, but I had to protect Jason also. "What could happen if a cat were to decide to climb the tree?" I asked, not quite ready to be totally relieved. I wouldn't be until we'd seen his reaction to the tree. In the past, I'd put up a small artificial tree and set it on a library table. Jason had been curious and even jumped up on the table a few times but never assaulted that tree.

He didn't take well to change. He'd finally accepted Chuck some time ago, but I couldn't predict how this new addition to our home would go. Would Chuck be okay with putting the tree in the front yard if Jason objected to its presence?

Brit tilted her head, considering how to respond. "I can't guarantee the safety of your tree once it leaves here, but on the other hand, I've only heard of a few instances of dissatisfied pets. Now children are a different story. They're much more unpredictable."

"Jason will do just fine," Chuck told me. "He and I had a long, serious talk while you were gone today, and I'm pretty sure he'll come around."

Was that what the ribbon necklace Jason greeted me with had been for? He hadn't seemed particularly keen on it. "Okay. Let's do this, then."

Brit's staff helped us prepare the tree for transport and tie it atop Chuck's car. Chuck put the tree stand on the back seat, and I carried the gallon jug of cider Brit had given us as a gift to the front seat. All in all, a satisfactory experience.

Time would tell whether Jason agreed.

CHAPTER 15

"I can only give you twenty minutes," Carol McGiver said first thing Monday morning when we showed up at her office.

"This is a homicide investigation, Ms. McGiver," Herc said in his official capacity. "We'll take whatever time it takes to get your input about the death of Terry Seiser."

A blue-eyed ash blond, she nodded like someone who recognized when her officious tone wasn't appreciated but still intended to stick to her own schedule. "He was murdered? I hadn't heard."

I couldn't believe Garvey hadn't called her as soon as we left her place on Saturday so they could get their stories together.

"In that case, please, have a seat, both of you," she said. "I'll help however I can."

Herc took the lead. "We've been told you're the one who handles the fundraising for Project Phoenix. What exactly has that involved?"

She placed her folded hands on her desk and leaned forward as if she couldn't wait to enlighten us about her work for low-income families. "I don't really handle that function anymore since Ellen Garvey came on board. Now, I'm the primary administrator of the Project, bringing the construction of new lower-cost housing to fruition. Ellen's financial contributions have allowed me to employ a small support staff, but she has become the voice of our fundraising efforts."

"How are those coming along?" I asked.

"Slower than I hoped, because there are so many people needing homes, but we are making progress. Thanks to Ellen's help, we've already built four lower-income houses just south of downtown and we have another four underway. Hopefully, despite Saturday's terrible accident, uh, murder, we'll still have contributors. We won't have those numbers for a few days."

"It sounds like your efforts are bearing fruit," I said, giving her her due.

She was gracious enough to smile. "Thank you. We've been working hard, especially the last six months."

"What can you tell us about Ellen Garvey?" Herc asked, growing impatient with the small talk.

"Ellen? Why do you want to know about her?"

"Just answer the question, please," Herc said.

She lifted her shoulders like there was nothing to tell. "Ellen has been our savior. Ever since the day we met, she has been nothing but helpful to me and to this project."

"How did that happen?" I continued.

"She'd wrecked her bike. I was driving by, stopped and gave her a ride home."

"Did you know who she was when you stopped?"

"No."

"Do you always stop for strangers?"

"No, of course not. But you've seen Ellen. She looked harmless, especially with a broken bike."

"And you had no idea she was the famous philanthropist?" Herc asked.

"No. Are you suggesting I was stalking her and took advantage of her situation?" She'd raised her voice, incensed that we'd even suggest such a thing.

"In your own words, Ms. McGiver, you were the main one

doing fundraising for your project until you met her. If you were any good at your job, you would've known who she was and what she could do for your cause."

She opened her mouth as if to protest and then closed it. "Okay, you got me. I did know who she was when I stopped. I couldn't believe my luck. But I didn't recognize her until I stopped. I wasn't trailing her like some of those with open hands do. I've seen it happen more than once since I met her. Some people appear to have no sensitivity when it comes to asking for money."

Her apparent incomprehension of the similarity between her story and the moneygrubbers she'd just described impressed me. Either she was that clueless or a very good actress. I couldn't decide at this point.

"How were you involved with the Reindeer Run?" Herc asked.

"After Ellen told me she wanted to sponsor some major event to raise funds for Project Phoenix, we spent several days brainstorming what that might be. Once we decided on a marathon around the holidays, I returned to everyday oversight of the project, and she took over planning the event."

"We understand a guy by the name of Cyrus Milligan came on board as a consultant on marathons," I said. "How well do you know him?"

"Not well. Only in regard to the marathon. I'd not met him before Ellen brought him on board, saying we needed someone on our team who really knew the ins and outs of putting on a race, since no one else on the committee other than Martin Brockhurst's brother, Wally, was very familiar with marathons. Martin is Ellen's financial advisor. Every so often in the last few months, she'd have me sit in with the rest of the small team who were planning the event."

"Were you present when the idea of constructing a viewing platform came up?" Herc asked.

"Oh, yes," she said with a tone that indicated she wanted to keep as much distance between that subject and her part in it.

"Who proposed it?" he continued, reacting to the inflection in her voice.

"Cy." She snorted, as if laughing at her own comment. "It all sounds so amateurish now, doesn't it? Holding such a big event with very little experience to help us know what we were doing."

"You depended on this Cyrus Milligan to be your guide?" I asked.

"Biggest mistake of all," she replied.

"Why do you say that?"

She picked up a ballpoint pen on her desk and rolled it between her fingers. "He rarely seemed to be on top of things even though his know-it-all attitude would have you believe otherwise. Ellen or someone else on the committee would ask him a question and he'd promise to investigate and get back to them. He liked to take credit for suggesting the viewing stand, even though Terry seized onto it as his project. Rarely was there any follow-through from Milligan, although no one seemed to hold him accountable, except Martin when it came to expenses. Ellen's lucky to have that man looking out for her money. That isn't her forte."

She definitely didn't like the consultant. Was it the ego she'd mentioned, or perhaps he was taking up more of Garvey's time than she liked? "Could you expand on why you say he liked to take credit for the idea?" I asked.

"Ellen wasn't crazy about it at first. I'm guessing because she had an inkling of how much it might cost and take away from the funds devoted to the project. But Milligan got really excited about how it could add a certain pizzazz to the race. His word, which should give you an idea how his mind works. He made it sound like the uniqueness of the stand would draw even more partici-pants to the race. It was Seiser who suggested it be constructed in such a way to be taken down and used over and over for other civic events. That's what got Ellen's approval."

I rephrased what she'd just told us. "Even though Milligan is the one who sold the idea to Ms. Garvey, Terry Seiser was the one who ran with it. Correct?"

"Yes."

"Why do you think that was?"

She shrugged. "Perhaps because up to that point he hadn't said much as a committee member. Ellen and Milligan had done most of the talking. I got the impression he was feeling left out and wanted to get back into the thick of things."

"Did he offer to provide the materials at that point?" Herc asked.

She took her time considering. "No, not then. That part came later, the day Milligan presented a plan he'd borrowed from some other event he'd found on the internet. That was maybe a week later, when our planning team met next."

"What was the reaction of Ms. Garvey and Milligan?" I asked.

"Milligan wasn't exactly pleased. I got the impression he may have already worked out a deal on the side with someone else. But Ellen jumped at Terry's offer. My guess is that she wanted to let Terry feel like he was more a part of things. That was before the actual price ever came up and before he backed away from just donating things. But by then, the idea was so far along, she didn't have much choice but to pay him, or rather, his hardware store and lumberyard."

We'd gone beyond the twenty minutes she said she'd give us, but she was making no sign she needed to leave. We had to keep going because we hadn't finished learning what she knew about Seiser.

I sent Herc a knowing look, and he took it from there. "Let's talk some more about Terry Seiser. How well did you know him?"

"Hardly at all. Ellen and I first met him shortly after she joined my project. She accompanied me on a trip to solicit both funds and materials from local merchants for the first four homes we were building. He was ready to turn me down outright until he noticed Ellen. She's a lovely, good-looking woman. No mystery there why he gave her a second look. The mystery to me was her reaction. The man was rude, and yet she was ready to overlook his attitude when he started paying attention to her."

"Did you see him much after that day?" I asked.

"Not right away. Maybe a month later she referred to something she and Terry had done a few days before. When I offered a curious look, she attempted to downplay her association with him. It was only after we started planning the marathon that he joined the team. Like I said, he didn't speak up much in the meetings, but he'd do things to let the rest of us know he and she were a thing and he had every right to be there. Things like touching her forearm every so often, sitting next to her and leaning in to whisper occasionally."

"When did you learn that Ellen had agreed to reimburse him for the materials he donated for the platform?" Herc asked.

"About a week before the race, and only then because she let something slip and I called her on it. Personally, I was angry, because I thought all along the platform was a frivolous idea, but when I heard that, I was disappointed because the money spent on it wouldn't go toward the project. But before you ask, no, I didn't tell her how I felt. She'd already done so much for my project."

"Where were you early Saturday morning?" I asked.

"I was still at home when the collapse occurred. I hadn't planned to go to the park until shortly before the race began. We'd set up a small tent outside where I'd oversee the revenue collected from late sign-ups at the entrance."

"When did you hear about the collapse?" Herc asked.

"As soon as I arrived at the park. I stuck around the rest of the morning waiting to hear if the event was postponed or canceled. Either way, there were a lot of cleanup and administrative details to handle. I didn't leave until a little after eleven, when the race was postponed until further notice."

A quick glance at her watch signaled her readiness to answer questions was coming to an end.

Herc gave her his card and the usual request to call him if additional details occurred to her.

He didn't start the car immediately. Instead, he pulled out his phone and checked his missed calls.

"What's up?" I asked. "Does Janet have a report already?"

"Nah, although I suspect she worked the rest of the weekend. This is personal."

Apparently he didn't find what he was looking for because he shoved his phone back in his jacket pocket.

What was up? My first thought was that it was medical. I constantly worried about his diet and lack of exercise. I shouldn't. I wasn't his mother. But I was his friend, and if he needed my support right now, I was ready to give it. "Want to talk about it?"

"Thought you were anxious to dissect the interview we just conducted?"

"I am, but if there's something on your mind that's keeping you from focusing on this case, you need to tell me so I can help you get past it."

He twiddled his fingers on the steering wheel. "It's not that big a deal. At least for you. I just, uh, followed through on one of your gift suggestions for Luann. This guy's supposed to call me back yet today."

I breathed out. "You had me worried, pal. Your expression got so intense."

"Sorry. This is just … important to me."

"Got it. What did you decide to do? Can you share that tidbit?"

"It's a destination gift. Mount Dora is known for antique stores. The old downtown is supposed to have lots of shopping and restaurants. I'm trying to get us reservations at this B&B during one of the big events coming up in January. The guy could get me one room, but we're not quite there yet, and I didn't want to scare her off. He's checking on the availability of a second room."

"Herc! That's so romantic. Luann is sure to love it."

"I hope so. Just so she hasn't already scheduled something else for that time. The chief is always sending her off to conferences and training he doesn't want to attend."

"Can't you call him and check?"

"Thought of that and rejected it. He's like a kid when it comes to secrets. And I really want this to be a surprise."

Poor Herc. He really had it bad. I was happy for him, but at the same time I felt for him with the agony he was putting himself through.

Time to change the subject. "Carol McGiver seems real enough and her work for low-income families and friendship with Ellen Garvey genuine."

"But there was something going on between her and that consultant," Herc replied, having returned to his investigator persona. "She doesn't like him."

"Nor did Seiser, if you believe her account of their team meetings. But enough to make him a suspect in the murder? We don't know enough about him yet."

"Want to track him down next?" he asked.

"Yes. If we can believe Carol McGiver's impression of him, we need to catch him before he leaves town."

CHAPTER 16

Cyrus Milligan was completely different from the person I envisioned. Bad habit, picturing a potential suspect before ever meeting him. Not good for a cop. My only excuse is that I'm no longer really a cop and interior designers are allowed to envision the unknown. In fact, they're expected to.

Anyway, since the guy was supposed to be an expert on race marathons, I figured he'd look like my idea of a runner: thin and muscular. Cyrus Milligan cleared five seven, if that much. Given the crinkles around his eyes and forehead, he looked to be in his fifties at least. No sweats or athletic garb for him. Instead, he wore a black long-sleeved tee and black jeans with a purple paisley scarf around his neck.

"Thanks for coming in today, Mr. Milligan," Herc said as he ushered the marathon consultant into the small conference room at the station.

"Since my job is just temporary, I've been using my motel room as my office. This works better for meetings like this. Ellen Garvey let me know you'd be seeking me out for information about the race sooner or later. In anticipation of your visit, I've put together this file for you." He handed Herc a manila folder. "I can send it electronically, if you prefer. I stuck my latest version of the design plan for the viewing stand in there."

We didn't often run into persons of interest who were seemingly ready for us with so much data. *Beware of sharks being too prepared to work with the police.*

"Latest version of the design plan?" Herc asked. "Did it get changed often?"

Milligan sat back in his chair and folded his hands in his lap. "I think this is the fourth iteration. It started off as a very sketchy idea with estimated dimensions. I had an engineering pal take a shot at it and then presented it to Ellen and the others. Seiser took it from there. Didn't appear to want my help or anyone else's so I left him alone. I had more than enough to handle with the rest of the run."

"We were told you were the one who first suggested having a viewing platform," I said. "Where did that idea come from?"

He left his comfortable position resting against the chair back and leaned forward, elbows on the table between us and his face resting in his hands. "Let me think. I'd heard through the grapevine that Ellen wasn't afraid to fire people who weren't delivering for her. At least that's what happened to her finance people. I felt I had to do more than just advise. I had to help her make the marathon memorable." He stopped, having realized what he'd just said. "Sorry, no slight to the deceased. Obviously I never figured the very thing I thought would do it would be the cause of another's death."

He'd given us a very safe response. I wasn't satisfied. "That's why you proposed it, but where did the idea come from? Had you seen it done somewhere else?"

"I sifted through several ideas in my head before I mentioned the platform. Fancier technology with which others could track various runners. Running clothes provided by famous fashion designers. Helicopter reporting. It had to be something that fit with Ellen's ethos but also splashy to gain attention. She doesn't mind being seen as the spokesperson for the cause, but she's not in it to make herself look good.

"I remembered being dragged to a campaign speech of some politician running for mayor in a town near Tampa. I'd been struck not necessarily by his words, but by how the man's team had presented him so appealingly on a platform built in a small park near the downtown. I guess that thought had been floating around in my brain for ages, just waiting to be implemented."

Interesting, if what he'd told us was the truth. He'd never seen it done in other races.

"Who actually built the viewing stand?" Herc asked.

"Seiser took over that part. I offered to oversee the small crew he hired, but he was having none of that. As soon as Ellen approved the concept, he grabbed onto it and didn't let go."

Now we were getting to the crux of the matter. Herc wasn't ready to move on. "Did you ever visit the race site as the platform was being built?"

"Sure. I was curious. It only took a few days to go up. But Seiser had put a cover over it, along with warning signs to keep away. Wouldn't let me near it when I called out to him under all that canvas."

"Did you discuss progress with him otherwise?" I asked.

"Tried to. So did Ellen, because I was there two days before when she asked him if it would be ready in time."

"And his response?"

"He essentially told me it was none of my business when I asked. He offered a broad smile, unusual for him, to Ellen and reassured her everything was on track. He vowed to give her a special private viewing the day before the race."

"It sounds like you and Mr. Seiser didn't get along," Herc said.

"You picked up on that, huh? You're right. We never got into a physical fight or even argued that much. We just didn't agree on very much. He was seeing Ellen socially. What she saw in him, I don't know. I got the feeling he didn't know either, which was why he did everything he could to stay close to her."

"How did she feel about that?" I asked.

"Like I said, I have no idea what she saw in him, but she was insistent he be part of the planning committee. Whether that was her own idea or his, I couldn't say."

"Where were you early Saturday morning?" Herc asked, getting around to Milligan's alibi.

"Nowhere near that platform, if that's what you're asking. I stayed late at the Rendezvous the night before, but still made it out of bed by five so I could get to the race in time to help the volunteers handling the start of the race. I was over there when word spread about the accident. That's what we thought it was at the time. I commandeered one of the golf carts the volunteers were using and headed over there in time to see the first responders."

"Did you inspect the remnants of the platform, either then or since?" Herc asked.

"Yeah. Can you blame me? My brilliant idea was now a pile of rubble. I ventured over there Saturday afternoon. The police guard standing watch allowed me within five feet of the debris when I explained who I was. They wouldn't let me any closer."

"What did you conclude from looking at it?" Herc asked.

"Truthfully, I couldn't believe it was an accident. I'd been over that design plan several times. Safeguards to prevent that very thing had been designed in."

"We'll leave things there for today," Herc said. "We may have additional questions once we've studied what's in the folder. Are you planning to stay in town, now that the race is on hold?"

"My motel bill has been prepaid for a few more weeks in anticipation of race wrap-up details, but I've got a new client in Texas I need to check in with."

"If you do leave town, we ask that you provide us with a forwarding address, at least until after the holidays, just in case we have additional questions," Herc said.

Milligan didn't look pleased, but he didn't object.

We took off for the car. "What did you make of that guy?" Herc asked once we were inside.

"Not sure. He seemed too helpful, but I can't figure out why."

"Trying to hide his real feelings about Seiser?" Herc said.

"Maybe, although he didn't attempt to make them sound like buds. Clearly, the two were angling for Ellen Garvey's attentions. But I'm not sure Milligan's feelings for her were/are romantic. Perhaps Seiser's claim on her pushed Milligan into a reactive mode."

"Milligan knew how that contraption was put together. Probably more than anyone else other than Seiser and the engineers he mentioned. He's the most likely person to tear it down."

"We need some background info on the guy. The kind Janet Oliver is so adept at finding," I said.

"Want to go back to the station and peruse this folder before we find that financial advisor?" he replied.

"I'm as anxious as you to look at that design plan, but I think we should talk to this Brockhurst guy as soon as we can. The whole point of the Reindeer Run was to raise funds for Project Phoenix. I don't want to give him additional time to reconsider Ellen Garvey's financial situation."

"Okay. A quick stop at the station to find Oliver and then we talk to this financial advisor," he said.

CHAPTER 17

Martin Brockhurst worked out of his condo, a very fashionable condo in a downtown high rise. A few months ago, Herc and I had nearly been incinerated in a fire on a higher floor in the same building. In fact, that's when Herc became interested in Luann, when she'd investigated the cause of the fire.

He walked us back to his office. "I've been expecting you. Ellen called me Saturday night and told me you'd be asking about her finances, in particular, her contributions to Project Phoenix."

If nothing else, Ellen Garvey was efficient, preparing those most closely associated with the race for our visits. Ninety-five percent of my investigator brain appreciated her efforts; five percent questioned if perhaps she was being too helpful. And if that little five percent proved correct, why?

Appearance-wise, Brockhurst was everything I imagined a financial advisor to look like: tall, slender, well-trimmed black hair, deep-set brown eyes and high forehead. In all, a very attractive man. Why had Garvey gravitated to Seiser instead of this man?

His office didn't disappoint, either. The color scheme was predominantly cream with black and dark brown accents. His steel desk held several neat stacks of documents and folders. Had he brought us here to maintain his distance by isolating himself behind his desk or to intimidate or impress us with his professional status?

He picked up a flash drive on his desktop and handed it to Herc. "Here's the financial data she asked me to provide you." We all took seats, Herc and I in the two black visitor chairs in front of his desk and Brockhurst in an oversize white leather manager chair. "Now then, what questions do you have for me?"

"Tell us about your relationship with Ellen Garvey," Herc began.

He raised a brow. "I thought you were investigating the Seiser murder, now that it's been deemed a homicide and not an accident?"

"We are," he replied. "But from what we've learned, you were connected to Mr. Seiser through Ellen Garvey."

"Oh. Sure. Makes sense. I've been working for Mrs. Garvey, Ellen, about three years. She'd been left a wealthy widow by her late husband, Neils. She probably told you he'd made his fortune from creating a chain of convenience stores where gas stations used to be. As a fourth-grade teacher, she'd been blissfully unaware of the bad feelings his business dealings had caused in the communities he touched until after his death. She tried to run the business herself for a while, but all the negatives he'd created kept rearing up their heads to challenge her."

"How long ago was this?" I asked, since Garvey had skipped over this part when we interviewed her.

"He died about five years ago. She struggled with running the business about a year, but you may have noticed Ellen was never cut out for that type of thing. She finally sold the business for a handsome profit. That was on top of the hefty estate he left her. In the meantime, she went through two accounting types before she found me. They helped her balance the books, but they had no idea what she should do with all her riches. That's when I came along. Well, she found me. Through recommendations of friends, my other clients."

"How would you describe your relationship?" Herc asked.

Again, he returned a confused look, but this time he didn't question our question. "Friendly. She respects my opinions about her finances, although I wish she didn't want to give so much away to her charitable activities." He must've realized how negative that sounded, so he quickly corrected himself. "Not that I have anything against philanthropy. But in order to keep giving, one must do so incrementally so they continue to have principal to invest."

"How well did you know Terry Seiser?" Herc asked.

"Not well at all. I wasn't an official member of the marathon planning committee, but on occasion Ellen has asked me to sit in on meetings to report on the event's finances, which wasn't easy because all I had to go on were the revenue and expenditures. That's the only time I interacted with the man."

"Did you like him?" I asked, since he'd been careful to only answer the specific question Herc had asked.

"No. Not at all. He didn't encourage friendships, not that I would have wanted to befriend him. He had a caustic personality. Unfortunately, Ellen didn't appear to see that. I saw him taking advantage of her and was afraid he'd help himself to her fortune. As it was, she wound up paying for the materials he initially said he'd contribute to building that platform."

"She said the plan was that she'd be reimbursed from whatever was collected by the Run," Herc said.

The very businesslike Martin Brockhurst rolled his eyes. "Supposedly. She has no idea how much that would cut into our proceeds. That's why she has me, but in this case, she wasn't listening. I despised him because of the influence he had over her but not enough to kill him, if that's what you're thinking."

"We're just trying to get a better feel for all the personalities and considerations involved," I said.

"You really think someone associated with the race or Ellen is responsible for his death?"

"They knew about the viewing stand," Herc replied.

"So did anyone else in the community who heard Ellen on TV last week. She was so proud of that special feature. She couldn't stop talking about it even though I don't think Seiser let her near it until a day or so before the event."

I gave myself a mental kick. I should've known Garvey would've done everything in her power to promote the race. Which meant anyone in Shasta or in viewing distance of that TV show could've slipped into the park and sabotaged the structure.

We were back to Square One.

"ARE YOU AS BUMMED AS I AM?" I ASKED HERC AS WE DROVE AWAY from Brockhurst's building.

"Because that guy just drastically widened our net of suspects?" he replied. "I'm more bummed that it should've occurred to me that the platform had been publicized before we spoke with him. We could've watched that interview on TV and checked the local news right away Saturday. Although I don't know how that would've helped this investigation."

"Let's go back to the station and look over the file Milligan gave us and the flash drive we got from Brockhurst," I said.

"Could we apply the brakes a bit? I feel the need of a hearty, sit-down lunch. Want to splurge?"

Hearty? Sit-down? His go-to meals when a case got to be too much was fast food. Drive-throughs. What was he up to now?

Since we were downtown already, we wound up at the Sunflower, an outdoor café. Not Herc's usual pick, but he read the menu with relish today. "Ever had a Mediterranean salad, Ro?" he asked.

"Every so often. Very refreshing. And healthy." Probably

shouldn't have added that last part. The salad didn't have a chance. But he surprised me and did order it.

I chose a Cobb salad instead. "What's up, Herc? This is entirely out of character for you. An open-air restaurant. Salad. Are you feeling okay?"

"Can't fool you, can I? While we were talking to the Brockhurst guy, I got a text from the owner of the B&B in Mount Dora. He hasn't been able to swing a second room. I've been excited about giving Luann this destination experience for Christmas, but I don't want to insult her with the offer of only one room. We're, uh, not quite there yet."

"Why the salad? To punish yourself? I'd think you'd be ordering a thick steak to take your mind off giving up on this present."

The look he gave me reminded me of the time when Val broke my favorite vase and attempted her most charming expression in hopes I either wouldn't notice or would decide not to punish her. "I, uh …" he mumbled.

"You haven't given up on the idea yet, have you?" I said, catching on. "Surely you're not hoping I'll talk you into going forward with it? If you don't feel comfortable about it, don't look to me to encourage you."

"But it was such a good idea, Ro. I already bought the tickets to the event."

"You could still attend that. Surely there's a motel in the area where you could reserve two rooms?"

He grimaced just like Val had when I told her she'd have to help pay for another vase. "You're right, but it just wouldn't be the same."

"Hercules Morgan, you've turned into quite the romantic."

"I just want to do something Luann won't forget."

"Why don't you reserve some rooms in a local motel in Mount Dora but keep this other reservation as long as the B&B owner will allow, just in case things between you and Luann progress faster than you think they will?"

"That's not a bad idea. Thanks, Ro!"

We wound up switching salads when he discovered his came without protein. He didn't place chickpeas in that category, and the chopped boiled eggs, sliced ham and chicken in mine were more appealing to him.

Lunch was a great mood-changer. Time to check in with Janet Oliver.

CHAPTER 18

"Fascinating reading material you brought me," Janet said when we caught up with her in the smaller conference room. "So much so I've been eating my lunch while I continued to sort through everything."

Her dedication to this case almost made me feel guilty for having eaten at the downtown open-air café. Almost, but not entirely. That Mediterranean salad really hit the spot. "What have you learned?" I asked, taking a seat across the table from her. "Anything with direct bearing on the collapse of the viewing stand?"

"Maybe not of direct bearing, but Ellen Garvey's finances are fascinating. She inherited millions from her late husband, and that was before she sold his company, which doubled her assets. There's a period right after his death where there was a steady flow of revenue out of her coffers. I'm guessing she didn't know how to handle that much money. But that turned around a little over three years ago. She started investing in stocks and bonds with surefire returns, and the bottom line has gradually been building up to its earlier amount."

"That's probably due to bringing Martin Brockhurst on

board," Herc said. He turned to me. "Apparently the guy really does know what he's doing."

"Which probably explains his attitude about the marathon and Garvey's other philanthropic endeavors," I said. "He sees them as counteracting all his good efforts to bring in more revenue."

"As for anything pertaining to this murder, my overall comment is that I don't see how the marathon and the Rendezvous raised much money for the charity, although not all the registration information has been counted yet."

I wasn't surprised. I'd been wondering how they could spend so much on the event and still make money from it. "I'm not familiar with how fundraising events are staged, but perhaps it takes more than the first year to start seeing significant returns."

"Maybe," she replied, "but I question how this event will be able to recover enough to see another year. But like you, Mrs. Summerfield, I don't have much experience with fundraising."

"Did you detect any signs of fraud or malfeasance?" Herc asked.

She checked her notebook computer before replying. "Nothing that jumped out at me, but I didn't find a project budget except a few sketchy comments from their committee meeting notes and no sign at all of purchasing procedures. When all the dust dies down, whoever goes over the books may well find problems."

"Thanks, Janet," I said. "Were you able to go through the folder we received from the marathon's consultant, Cyrus Milligan?"

"I briefly went through it and didn't find any recommendations about adopting strong financial procedures from him. Even if such procedures were not considered by Mrs. Garvey, I would think that would be one of the key tasks of the consultant."

"Did you find evidence of other 'bright ideas' being discussed before they landed on the idea of a viewing stand?" Herc asked.

"I haven't finished reviewing their meeting minutes, although sometime in October Milligan brought up that idea."

"What kind of discussion did it produce?" I asked.

"A lot of preliminary questions like what other marathons used viewing stands, how would one benefit the race and estimated cost. Milligan hedged on those. Gave the appearance of answering each without providing any specifics."

Herc started reading through the folder. "Not even about cost?"

"You should read that part for yourselves. It's classic non-speak. He couched his response on whether they could obtain donations from benefactors."

"Speaking of donations, besides whatever Ellen Garvey was contributing, did they plan for additional revenue other than participant fees and ticket sales?" I asked.

"Not that I've run across yet," she answered. "You'd think Milligan would have suggested something like sponsors. Garvey's money should have served only as seed money for the event so as not to deplete her funds the first year."

"Sounds like Milligan wasn't contributing his fair share to the planning. Or perhaps he wasn't all that competent," Herc said. "Have you been able to uncover anything else about the guy, Janet?"

She shook her head, her expression downcast as if the lack of information about the man was her fault. "Just what he has on his website, which is mainly a list of races in which he's run, no mention of placements, by the way, and a glowing list of services he can provide, all in such general terms the reader can't decide if he's offering to paint your house, raise your children or help plan a marathon."

"No mention of prior experience? Testimonials?" I asked.

"Nothing."

I turned to Herc. "Ellen Garvey's track record picking competent people to run the marathon keeps going down in my eyes."

"Track record? Good one, Ro," Herc replied.

"Sorry, I hadn't meant to pun. At least she's got Martin Brockhurst on her team. And Carol McGiver. They both seem to be legit," I replied.

"Well, yes and no," Janet said. "I've found more background data on Brockhurst than Milligan. He grew up in a small town in New Jersey until he was thirteen, when his father, an entomologist, took a job with an orange grove not far from here. Brockhurst and his brother, Wally, who is two years younger, went to public schools. Both attended the University of Central Florida, Brockhurst getting his degree in accounting."

I recalled Ellen saying the idea for the marathon had come from Brockhurst, whose brother was a runner. "How about the brother, Wally? Did you find anything on him?" I asked.

Janet grimaced like I'd just stepped on her foot. "Not much. He appears to have dropped out of school after two years and got involved in amateur sports wherever a hefty pot was involved. Couldn't find much about his winnings, if any even existed. He lives here in Shasta but not with his brother."

I thought about my sister, Claire, who lived in Miami. She was an emergency room nurse who rarely got much time off, so we didn't see each other much. But we still had what I considered a good relationship. A good long-distance relationship anyhow. "How do the two get along?" I asked. "Were you able to find anything about that?"

She broke into a smile. Apparently this time she had something to report. "There are several photos of the two of them together on the internet. Vacationing, water skiing, fishing. Given the changes in their hairstyles, I'd say the shots were taken over a period of years. They might hate each other, but at least they've been spending time together and memorializing it on the internet."

Herc had been staring at me since I asked my question. "Why would Martin Brockhurst even suggest a marathon if he wasn't getting along with his brother?"

I pulled on my ear, like I hoped my brain waves might connect with the lobe. "I'm not sure. Maybe I wasn't thinking so much about their relationship as Wally's financial situation. If the guy had been struggling, his brother might have suggested a race just to give Wally a boost in that area. However, if Wally had been doing all right, Martin might have been thinking more about the good of the project."

"Either way, once Martin Brockhurst brought the idea of a marathon to the table, he didn't advocate for it. Garvey told us she's the one who jumped on it, partially because the team was running out of planning time and because she liked the healthy, outdoor feature," Herc said.

"Good point, Herc." I switched my attention back to Janet. "Anything else you've learned about Brockhurst?"

Other research assistants might have taken offense that I didn't appear to be satisfied with the already proven extent of her efforts, but Janet Oliver was not like other research assistants. She was accustomed to our insatiable need for data. And she also was seriously considering becoming one of us. Plus, I'd learned she tended to save the best for last, like a chef with her pièce de résistance.

"As a matter of fact, there is one more item you should know about. Remember the internet photos I cited? I didn't mention there were a couple of the two brothers working on some construction project. Not just putting together a kit for a piece of furniture but actually on the roof of a house, hammering away on the shingles."

Both Herc and I sat forward. "Do you have those on your computer?" Herc asked.

"Sure do. I thought you might want to see them up close and personal," she replied.

There was no mistaking it was Martin Brockhurst in the two photos. The guy next to him had to be his brother, as much as he resembled Martin. They could've been posing for some sort of publicity shot, but their sweat-stained faces suggested otherwise.

"What do you know? Martin Brockhurst appears to have some experience in construction," I said.

"We appear to have another bona fide suspect," Herc said.

"I don't disagree, but what's the motive?" I asked.

"Jealousy? Maybe he didn't have feelings for Ellen Garvey, but seeing all his efforts to enhance her finances being eaten up by her charitable inclinations may have forced him to take a stand to stop them."

"But Herc, killing Seiser and thus ending the marathon wouldn't end her philanthropic tendencies," I said.

"But it might slow them down," he replied.

"True. Maybe that's why he was so ready with that thumb drive. He hoped it would answer our questions so we'd forget about him."

"So much for that ploy," Herc said. "As far as I'm concerned, the spotlight is back on him."

CHAPTER 19

We thanked Janet for all her hard work and then outlined the rest of our day. We had to get as much accomplished interview-wise today before the trail grew even colder. But first I wanted to check in with Val, who was working on finishing touches at Mehaffy House.

"This is looking incredible," I told her and meant it once I entered the house. I tried not to feel guilty for all the time I'd neglected this project, what with this case and the one before it. After all, I was serving the public good in catching the killers, and I'd left her, Ryder and the crew excellent design plans. Which, coincidentally, was the reason I'd wanted to stop off here before beginning our interviews.

"Thanks, Mom. That means a lot coming from you. But I suspect there's more behind this visit than to inspect our progress."

I turned to Herc. "I raised a smart one, Herc. She catches right on."

"I've been telling you that for years," Herc said, beaming at my daughter.

Before we left the station, I'd made a copy of the design plan for the viewing platform. I offered Val the folder containing that document. "In your spare time, could you and Ryder take a look at this?" I told her what it was. "I tried to interpret it, but I want to get your opinion about how it was to be constructed before I draw a conclusion."

She stared at me warily. "Since when can you not interpret schematics?"

"I just want to be sure. I know you're all anxious to finish up this project before the holidays, but this should only take a few minutes of your time. Let me know as soon as you can."

We pivoted to head out.

"Wait, Mom. Before you go, you haven't given me any clues what you'd like for Christmas."

"I didn't think we were exchanging this year," I replied, which is what I'd been saying for years and then ignoring our agreement to stop and gifting her anyway.

"Right, like you ever pay attention to that deal. Speak now or soon, or it'll be another gift card."

"Good. I like gift cards," I said, debating whether she'd pick my favorite online department store or the bookstore in town. Either way was fine with me.

"I like gift cards, too," Herc added.

"Right. You wouldn't be happy unless I got you your annual bottle of scotch," Val said.

"See? I told ya. She's the smart one in the family," Herc told me as we left.

"I already have your gift card to Bohannon's restaurant," I answered good-naturedly. "Like you get every year. If you don't like eating there anymore, you've got to let me know sooner than a couple days before Christmas."

"So you have been holiday shopping," he said. "You haven't said a thing about what you've been up to."

"I've been too interested in your holiday problems."

"Oh. Sorry. Anything you want to run by me? Like what to get Deli Man."

I smiled mysteriously. "Not to worry. I've got that under

control."

By now we'd reached the car. "What does one buy for a guy who owns a deli, a restaurant and a wine bar?"

"Good question. I think I finally figured out the answer."

"So?"

He could be such a kid when it came to Christmas. But I wasn't ready to share. "You'll have to wait until Christmas. It won't be long. And it's getting even closer as we waste time discussing it instead of the case."

WE FOUND JOSHUA COLLINS, SEISER'S ATTORNEY, AT HIS OFFICE, A one-man operation downtown. Completely bald, wearing round eyeglasses, he glanced up from his laptop as we came through the door. "You're the police, right? Come to find out what you can from me about the estate of the late Terry Seiser?"

I took him to be somewhere in his late sixties or early seventies.

"Yes," Herc said and introduced himself. "This is Rowena Summerfield, who consults with us on certain cases."

"Morgan and Summerfield, huh? Never met either of you, but I've heard things through the grapevine. You seem to have a pretty good reputation."

"Thanks. We've been at it several years."

"You could say the same for me, although I've got a decade or more on you both. I'm more a family attorney. I was an old buddy of Bill Seiser when he was first getting started with his hardware store. As a favor, I agreed to represent him both personally and in his business. For reasons unknown to me, young Terry kept me on as his attorney when his dad passed. It was purely a business arrangement. We didn't care much for each other then, nor did that situation change up to this past Saturday."

One more *glowing endorsement* of the dead man. "How do you account for that relationship?" I asked.

He eyed me like he might study a witness for the other side. "Does that really matter, Mrs. Summerfield, or am I a suspect in your investigation?"

Though his eyes bore into mine, daring me to back down, this wasn't my first rodeo, especially with attorneys. "Actually, it does matter, Mr. Collins. Your client seems like he had more enemies than friends. We came here today to discover what we could about the health of the business and the victim's private affairs. You're the one who suggested you might have your own ax to grind."

Herc made an imperceptible movement forward only I noticed. I'd gone too far too soon. "At this point, you're not a suspect, Mr. Collins. Nor even a person of interest, other than what you can tell us about Mr. Seiser's legal affairs."

Collins relaxed his shoulders, which had risen with my question. "Terry was an only child. For all Bill's good points, he wasn't one to rein in the kid after the mother ran out on them. Terry had just become a teenager, and the loss of his mother affected him more profoundly than the kid would admit. He acted out his grief, made life miserable for his dad. Because Bill didn't hold the kid accountable for his actions, Terry just kept testing the waters more."

"Are you saying his late father is responsible for the man Terry Seiser became?" Herc asked.

Collins held up a hand. Herc had gone too far. "No. We're all responsible for our own lives, but it didn't help that the young Seiser started out with a chip on his shoulder. He must have thought his dad and thus his meal train would go on forever. Bill's sudden death threw him. Suddenly, Terry owned the hardware store and the recently acquired lumberyard. He was accustomed to having everything paid for by them, but having to manage them was a real shocker."

"We understand Seiser worked in the store before his father died," I said. "Did he not learn anything from that experience?"

"You'd think so, wouldn't you?" Collins replied. "But from

what I observed during those days, Bill would slough off whatever mistakes or bad behavior the kid exhibited. He admitted to me once that he should have been sterner but was afraid Terry would go off on his own after high school, and he didn't want that. More than anything he wanted his son to take over for him someday so he could retire."

"But he never got that chance," Herc said. "He suffered his heart attack shortly after his son graduated from high school."

"Bill was a good man. And he tried to be a good father. But he never prepared himself or Terry for the possibility he could die young."

Collins had been forthcoming about the young Terry. Perhaps it was time to return to the relationship question. "Did you ever have a run-in with the kid while his father was still alive?" I asked, hoping rephrasing my question would produce a more definitive response.

He folded his hands on top of his desk and stared me down. "I know what you're doing, ma'am. But in this case, because I think you may have struck upon the key behind his death, I'll answer your question. But bear in mind, I said, 'may have.' I raised four kids myself. Always considered myself a pretty good father. They still keep in touch with me even though they're all off on their own with promising careers, so I speak with some authority. One time, after I'd witnessed Terry talking back to Bill, I took it upon myself to talk to the kid once his dad left the room. Bad idea. Told me in no uncertain terms to mind my own business."

I could almost picture the scene. Val had gone through a brief period where she rebelled against authority, but I held firm and she came through it within a few months. "Thank you for sharing that," I told him sincerely.

"Kept my distance after that. Just dealt with Bill until …"

"You no longer could," Herc said.

"Never underestimate the power of holding grudges," Collins said. "Terry Seiser could in particular, although he chose to keep me on for legal matters. Probably because he didn't want to take the time to find someone else. Or maybe he did and they were less sympathetic. Anyway, the first time we met as client and attorney, he questioned every paragraph in his father's will. Mainly, he thought he could put the place on the market, pocket the proceeds and walk away. Bill hadn't seen it that way. He left his estate in trust with me as its administrator until Terry turned thirty. Why Bill thought that was the magic number ensuring the kid's eventual maturity is beyond me."

"You administered the trust for several years?" Herc asked.

"Tried to. Soon learned I couldn't manage the hardware store and lumberyard and still maintain my private practice. I hired an accounting manager to watch the finances and a general manager for the store. The lumberyard was in pretty good shape under the then manager, who's since retired, so I left it alone."

"That's how it remained until he turned thirty?" I asked.

"Not quite. The young woman I hired to keep the books, Muriel Fox, has remained on until this day. Not the most personable woman, but she's efficient. When the lumberyard manager retired, I promoted the assistant manager. That's Gordo Zaharian. I assume you've either talked to him or you will. But Terry didn't get on with the hardware store manager, Roscoe Fridley, probably because the guy wouldn't put up with any of Terry's nonsense or smart remarks. By the time Fridley quit, Terry was in his late twenties. Tried to convince me he'd seen the light and wanted more than anything to step up to the plate and do the store proud."

"And you believed him?" Herc asked before I did.

"Not for a minute, but I relented for two reasons. First, I was tired of doing battle with him over every little penny he wanted to spend. It was time for him to learn the hard facts of financial life. And second, he wanted to get married. At first, the girl, woman, Jillian Bowles, seemed the answer to his prayers. Pretty, smart, and I heard from others she didn't put up with his attitude. During those years, she helped him with the business. It didn't exactly flourish, but they managed to keep it going."

Al had told us Seiser was once married until the woman left him. She'd later died. "What happened to her?" I asked, although I was aware of her death.

Collins raised a brow. "You don't know? Perhaps I can contribute something more than my feelings about the man to this interview. A few years after they married, they lost a child. Jillian went into a deep depression; Terry reverted to his old ways. She left him a year later and divorced him soon after." He sighed as one who was wont to finish his train of thought. "I heard through friends that she died five years ago."

Check her off our list of possible suspects. "Did they have any further contact after the divorce?" I asked.

"Not that I'm aware. I wouldn't characterize their divorce as amicable, but once she got her freedom and the financial settlement she wanted, she disappeared. Left town anyhow."

"And left the world with the charming guy who's now dead himself," Herc said.

Collin's gaze went from Herc to me like he was expecting another question. When neither of us spoke immediately, he filled in the void. He settled back in his chair, his arms placed comfortably on the arm rests. "Now that we've been through the preliminaries and niceties, let's talk about what you really came here for, the current state of Seiser's finances and who inherits what. Right?"

"Uh, yeah," Herc said.

"The hardware store is on the brink of bankruptcy. The lumberyard is doing better but not by much. Terry had been living with a double-edged sword; he couldn't manage his business, and he was greedy. Up until a few years ago, he didn't have a will. Didn't have any heirs, so he didn't care. Plus, like his dad, he lived his life like there'd always be another day to recoup his losses. A couple years ago, I finally convinced him to take care of the people who'd kept him afloat all these years, his housekeeper, Carmen Loomis, and his office manager, Muriel Fox."

"Were they aware of the will?" I asked. "Muriel Fox seemed to think she'd be taking over when we interviewed her."

"I couldn't say. Probably, because I wouldn't put it past Terry to let the idea dangle like a carrot to maintain her loyalty. Same for what he might've said to Carmen Loomis."

"In other words," Herc said, "both women just came up a notch as suspects on our list."

Collins shook his head, like he'd been waiting for just such a reaction. "Terry revised his will last month. He left everything to Ellen Garvey, the philanthropist."

I opened my mouth and closed it. Herc jerked in his seat.

Collins smiled the smile of the all-knowing Oz. "Cute, huh?"

"Did he say why?" I asked, still trying to get my brain around this twist.

"Not exactly. 'Let them chew on that,' he said. You got any idea what that meant?"

Herc scrunched up his eyes. "Sounds like he thought he was getting back at someone, but who?"

"Those two employees, of course," Collins said.

"Probably," I replied. "But I can't imagine Ellen Garvey would even want his business or home. What point was he trying to make? Surely he didn't think she'd even want those assets."

"It's possible Terry was just amusing himself with the women and intended to change things back eventually. Maybe he was playing a long game with all three," Collins said. "I didn't give it much thought at the time, because like him, I thought he'd be around long after I was gone and I wouldn't have to worry about giving those two women the bad news."

And now that contingency was a reality. "Do they know?" I asked.

"I haven't said anything to them yet. Technically, I don't have to," Collins replied, "since they are no longer named in the will. But from a humanitarian standpoint, it's probably necessary."

Neither of us spoke.

"Just find his killer fast," he said.

CHAPTER 20

couldn't wait to get in the car before I pumped Herc for his opinion about Collins. "What did you make of that?" I asked.

"Collins or what we learned from him?"

Typical stalling technique when he was still processing an interview.

My way of processing was to share my thoughts. "Collins himself was a bit of a surprise—his candor, that is. But I was mainly getting at what he told us, both about Seiser's background and his will."

"It's the recent change he made to his will that stuck with me," Herc said, opening his car door. "If he hadn't revised it and left everything to Ellen Garvey, I would've said either Fox or Loomis was our primary suspect. But now they're out of the running."

"But do they know that?" I said. "Let's say they did. The only reason they would've had for killing him would be for revenge. If they didn't, why now? Why did they think they needed the money now?"

"Either way, we need to talk to them right away."

"And spare Collins his difficult moments?" I said, only half kidding.

"He could always sit in with us, or vice versa, but that would probably be a conflict of interest."

"Fox first. She has more to lose."

Ten minutes later, we knocked on the door of the still-closed hardware store. It took several seconds before Fox appeared at the door. "We're clo— oh, it's you again. I told you everything I knew Saturday. Nothing's changed." She attempted to close the door, but Herc pushed back.

"Not so fast, Ms. Fox. We've got new questions," he said in his best professional tone.

Her shoulders collapsed, like she was giving up her attempt to shut out the rest of the world. "Okay, I want to help you find his killer. It's just that … the sky is falling in on me. Everything Terry put off doing over the years because it took too much time or skill or money is coming back to haunt me instead of him."

Time for a little compassion. I wasn't sure if it was warranted, but if it helped calm her down enough to talk to us, it was worth a try. "Can we go back to your office where you'd be more comfortable?" At her nod, I took it from there. "Do you want some coffee or perhaps water?" I asked when we'd all settled into the cramped space.

"Thanks, but it doesn't help. I could use a shot of whiskey, but I've got to keep my head straight."

"What all are you doing?" Herc asked at the sight of the stacks of ledgers and papers on her desk.

She licked her lips and kept rubbing her hands together as she settled into her chair. "I had things in pretty good order last Friday, at least according to the way Terry wanted things. But the IRS wants to meet tomorrow, and I'm not sure what to show them."

"The IRS has contacted you?" I said.

"Terry has been avoiding them for weeks, but when they called this morning, I'd run out of excuses."

The anticipation of a visit from the IRS can throw anyone into a tizzy, but she was exhibiting signs of apprehension that went deeper. She knew something. Something she didn't want the IRS, or us, to know. This was the time to push. "What have you and your late boss been hiding from the government, Muriel?" I asked.

She blinked several times. I thought she was about to burst into tears, but then she seemed to compose herself. "Hiding?" She attempted to laugh it off. "Nothing, really. But you never know what to expect from an official visit. And with Terry gone, we're especially vulnerable."

"Good try," I replied, "but there's more to your nervousness. Just what kind of 'visit' is this? Are they auditing your returns or following up on someone's complaint?"

She grabbed hold of the edge of her desk. To keep from rubbing her hands?

"W-why would you suggest either of those options?"

"That's usually what spurs a visit from them," Herc said. "Unless something else, something even more serious has brought them calling?"

"That's a ludicrous suggestion!" she returned so vehemently, she lost hold of her desk and started rubbing her hands together again.

"Look, Muriel"—I started calling her by her first name, hoping to lower the tension—"we're not the IRS. We're not here to audit, write up, chastise you or whatever. But your financial records, the books for the hardware store, that is, could be related to his murder. We need answers, definitive answers and facts, now so we can do our job."

She stopped rubbing her hands and placed one of them on her cheek. "I understand. I do, but as much as the man drove me crazy, I never pictured moving on without him. This whole situation is more than I can tolerate."

"What will the IRS find?" Herc asked, pulling on the loose thread.

Pursing her lips, she glanced away, apparently finding a bunch

of printouts attached to the corkboard on the wall more fascinating than us. "I'm not sure. And that's the truth."

"Could you elaborate on that for us?" Herc asked.

"The bottom line is that the hardware store is failing. We've
continued to bring in revenue, but less and less of that has shown
up on the books. I've done as much as I felt I could do to keep
things on the up and up without losing my job, but Terry learned
just enough about accounting and purchasing over the years to,
uh, write his own story."

"In other words, your boss was cooking the books?" Herc said.

She rolled her eyes. "Not the nicest way of putting it, but that's
the gist."

"Did you just suspect his interference, or did you know it for a
fact?" I asked.

"I should have an attorney present to answer that question.
Not that I'm guilty of anything, but I need to protect myself in
case the IRS finds something."

"Do you have an attorney?" Herc asked.

"I suppose Joshua Collins. He's represented the hardware
store for years."

It wasn't our place to tell her what we'd learned from Collins.
She'd find out soon enough. I changed the wording of my question. "Did you ever confront Mr. Seiser with your suspicions?"

She considered the question. "I probably shouldn't answer
that either. What I will say is that Terry wasn't an easy man to
work with. Even though I worked with him for years, I never
truly understood him."

"Did he ever threaten you?" I asked, it dawning on me that
besides now fearing prosecution by the IRS, she may have been
frightened by Seiser himself.

Her hands went back to gripping the front edge of the desk.
"Threaten me? Terry threatened all the time. Not just me. Everyone. It was his style."

I'd caught her off guard for some reason. She'd covered pretty well, although I'd noticed an almost imperceptible twitch in her eye. "What I meant was, did he ever threaten you physically?"

She blew out a breath. "No. He was the personification of his bark being worse than his bite. The recipient of his ire just had to withstand his wrath."

"Which it appears you learned how to do over the years," Herc said, attempting to draw her out.

"I've grown to love this job, as long as I didn't cross him, which was mainly a matter of avoiding him as much as possible."

Herc eyed her, trying to read between the lines. "Did he threaten you?"

She widened her eyes. "I didn't say that," she said huffily.

"Not in so many words, but you've gone out of your way to not to answer Mrs. Summerfield's question directly.

Was that Hercules Morgan taking a touchy-feely approach? He definitely had been spending too much time with me.

She rose. "Are we finished? As I've told you, I have mountains of paperwork to scale."

"Sit down, Ms. Fox," Herc said. "We've only just begun. We'll give you time to find an attorney where it concerns the books, but if you're not forthcoming soon about the hardware store's finances, I'll send one of my staff to go through the books with you."

"Can you do that?" she asked more timidly.

"Check with your attorney," Herc replied. "In the meantime, what can you tell us about your boss's participation in the Reindeer Run?"

"We covered that Saturday."

"Please," I intervened. "Could we go over that again, particularly how much of your inventory he was contributing?"

"As I told you, any time I asked about the store's participation in the event, he shut me out. I tried to keep tabs without him knowing. The only items that seemed to be contributed were small items—nails, hammers, nuts and bolts, wrenches. You'll need to talk to Gordo Zaharian about the other items, like lumber and other framework for the platform."

"How did you know even that much about the viewing stand, if he wouldn't discuss it with you?" Herc asked.

"From what I read in the paper and saw on the television interview."

"That was just last week," I said. "You didn't know about it until then?"

"No. I only suspected he was involved."

I eyed Herc. We hadn't gotten much more from her this morning other than the part about the IRS visit and the inkling that Seiser had threatened her in some way that she wouldn't discuss.

Herc took it from there. "That's all for now, until you've consulted an attorney, which I suggest be sooner rather than later. We need more information about his finances. In the meantime, there's a woman on my staff I'd be happy to assign to help you for a day or two, when you're ready to let us see the books."

We left her before she had a chance to reply.

"Collins has his hands full," Herc said once we were out of earshot.

"Because of the will?"

"That, too, but he must decide if he can continue to represent the store but not her. He's still Seiser's attorney from that stand-point. If she starts to look more like our killer, she'll need her own attorney."

"And from the way she kept hedging our questions, that contingency may well come to pass," I said. Dealing with one attorney was usually challenge enough. Dealing with two did not bode well.

CHAPTER 21

"I need more caffeine if we're gonna keep going today," Herc said. "There's a coffee shop just down the street."

For once, I wasn't up for coffee, so I took advantage of the season and ordered a hot cider instead, along with a sugar cookie.

Herc checked his phone for messages.

"Constantly checking your phone won't result in someone canceling their B&B reservation," I said.

"Am I that obvious?"

"Have you followed up on my suggestion to book a second place as your backup?" I asked, now feeling more like his big sister than his partner.

"Yeah." He didn't sound happy about it. Then he realized how he'd come across. "Sorry. You were just trying to help. Truth is, I shoulda made this arrangement long ago."

"But in your defense, you and Luann have only gotten … more friendly … recently."

"Thanks for that. I'm sure Luann will understand when I tell her how much I tried to make Plan A happen."

Oops. "Uh, not such a good idea. Just tell her about Plan B and don't call it that. She'll be just as thrilled. Because it's something that tells her you were thinking of her."

He set his phone back on the table and sipped his coffee. "Back to Muriel Fox. I don't know what to make of her. How 'bout you?"

"About the same. She initially came across, or tries to come across, as a woman totally in control. On top of things, devoted to the business. But after seeing her today, I'd say she's a woman who's been bound too tight now starting to unwind. Unable to control things with the business, she's still holding on as tight as possible to the way things were before Saturday."

He sipped some more, most likely running my assessment through his head. "Yeah, that sums it up pretty well."

"What do you plan to do about this IRS tie-in?"

"As much as I want to know about that store's finances, my gut tells me to leave the IRS out of this. At least until they come calling on us."

I debated whether to order another cookie, and my conscience won out. "She's worried, Herc. I'm guessing Seiser wasn't the only one who moved a few numbers around."

He screwed up his forehead. "Really? She struck me as the honest-to-a-fault type."

"Initially, me as well. But her resistance to my questions about Seiser threatening her was telling. I believe her when she says it wasn't physical. I'm thinking it was more of a personal nature. Not that she had feelings for him. No, her disgust with him was evident. But there was something else."

He leaned in. "Yeah? Like what?"

"She's never been married, but I think it might be something in her personal life. Something he knew about and used as leverage over her. Maybe she reached a point this past week, maybe because of the impending IRS visit, where she couldn't take it anymore."

"And killed him?" Herc took up his phone and starting

texting. "I'm asking Oliver to check into Muriel Fox's background while we move on to Carmen Loomis."

"Good idea," I said. "You should also consider assigning someone to watch her. She might decide the only way out is to run."

"Gotcha."

THE CARMEN LOOMIS WHO GREETED US AT SEISER'S FRONT DOOR WAS not the same woman we interviewed on Saturday. This woman had unearthed the stash of makeup we'd found hidden away on our last visit. She'd also changed from the drab housedress she'd worn earlier into a pair of black jeans and a tight-fitting red sweater. "I'm glad you came back, Lieutenant," she said with an artificial smile. "I wasn't myself the other day."

She invited us in to sit in the living room again. It, too, had been transformed. A large Christmas tree had been set up in a corner and decorated to the hilt. Other Christmas decorations had been placed about the room.

"Do you have more questions?" she asked.

"Just a few follow-up items," Herc replied. "I have to say, we're a bit surprised to see the place all decked out for the holidays so soon after Mr. Seiser's death. Has a date for a funeral even been set?"

"There isn't going to be one. His cousin has decided to keep things low-key whenever they release his body." She glanced about the room. "As for the holiday mood, Terry never celebrated Christmas or any other holiday. I felt the house needed some cheer. Would you like something to drink? I have coffee and can make tea."

We both refused. Had we not just had a coffee break, I'm not sure what Herc's reaction would've been. But I was spooked by her appearance and demeanor. A hot beverage didn't go with my mood.

"Did you ever discuss the Reindeer Run with Mr. Seiser?" Herc asked. It was a repeat of a question he'd posed on our first visit, but it was intended to get things started.

"Not per se. I don't think he ever mentioned it directly, but on more than one occasion, he told me he'd be late for dinner or to forget about dinner because he was meeting with the planning committee for a local event."

"Did you know what he was referring to?" I asked.

She chuckled. "Of course. In order to run this household effectively, I needed to be aware of whatever was going on in his life. Terry wasn't one to share much of anything with me, but that was his way. I didn't take offense."

"How did you find out?" I continued.

She offered what could only be described as a coy smile. "I had my ways."

In other words, she listened in on phone calls and checked his phone whenever he left it unattended. Not quite passive-aggressive. More just plain sneaky, a special brand of conflict avoidance. She hadn't felt she could ask him anything directly, so she resorted to less direct means.

"Tell us more about your relationship with Mr. Seiser," Herc said.

She held her hands out surrender-style. "What can I say? He was helpless when it came to anything about the house. He couldn't even attend to normal upkeep chores and early on had a fit when I hired out things like cutting the grass and changing light bulbs. I learned how to do them myself. I didn't mind. I liked that he depended on me."

"Did he show his appreciation of your services?" I asked.

She offered a blank expression. "I'm not sure I understand what you mean? He paid me on time and allowed me to live here rent-free. He gave me a household allowance, which I learned how to stretch as far as possible so that I could put aside a few pennies each month. Most nights, he came home. Those were his ways of showing his appreciation."

Was she putting us on? How could those actions possibly be interpreted as anything other than Seiser using her as far as she would tolerate?

"You said he came home 'most nights.' Where was he on the nights he didn't come home?" I asked.

Again, the blank expression, only this time there was a trace of something behind her eyes. Like she disapproved of something but didn't want to let on how she felt. "I used that expression because I went to bed at my usual ten o'clock time and he hadn't returned by then. He might have come in later in the night, but I didn't hear him."

Although I couldn't prove it, this woman had acute hearing. I just knew it. If there was something to be heard, like an inebriated Seiser returning home after a night on the town, she would've known. "What about his bed the next morning? Could you tell if it had been slept in?" I asked.

She glanced down. I couldn't tell if that was false modesty or she was hesitant to tell. "Sometimes I'd find it still made."

Herc's head was bobbing up and down. He was losing patience with this line of questions. "Had he been with women on those nights?"

She glanced away briefly. Her downturned expression when she returned our gaze was as if it pained her to talk about that part of his personal life. "I can't say for sure, but I detected the smell of cologne when I laundered the shirts he'd worn on those nights."

Herc didn't drop it. "How often did this happen?"

"Not often. Maybe once a month," she said. "Sometimes he'd go for months without, uh, seeing someone."

Herc gave me a high sign. Coward. My turn to twist the screw. "How about lately? Could you tell if he was seeing someone?"

"I think so, but some of those times were the meetings I mentioned earlier. And he never stayed out all night. He was usually home by eleven. Never later than midnight."

If she'd wanted to, I guessed she would've been able to

provide us with a complete list of dates and times when he'd been out. But she was still attempting to convince us Seiser's private life didn't matter to her.

Time to go for the jugular. "Was your relationship with Mr. Seiser ever anything other than employer and employee?" I asked.

Her hand went to her chest. "Me and Terry? No, how dare you suggest such a thing?"

I ignored her protest. "If nothing ever happened there, have you ever been involved with anyone else?"

She sat up straighter and folded her hands in her lap. "That is none of your business. I see no reason why my private life has anything to do with your investigation."

Herc decided to play bad guy now. "Ms. Loomis, thus far everything you've told us about your role in this household suggests your life revolves solely around running this house. It appears to have a strong emotional hold on you. We're merely trying to determine if there's more to your life."

She didn't speak for several beats. Neither Herc nor I moved or said anything further ourselves as we waited for her reaction.

Finally, she answered Herc. "I'm sorry if there's nothing juicy about my life to entertain your prurient interests, Lieutenant. I'm a widow. That part of my life ended years ago when I lost my husband."

She was attempting to shame us. Even if her life was every-thing she'd said it was, which I didn't believe, we were trained not to react. Although we'd pretty much covered as much terri-tory as we could today.

Herc appeared to take the high road. "We didn't mean to insult you, Mrs. Loomis. We're just attempting to do our job. Just a couple more questions. What are your plans now that your employer has died?"

"Plans? To stay here, of course."

Collins hadn't been here yet. But we had to be sure.

"Have you heard from Mr. Seiser's attorney yet?" Herc asked.

"Mr. Collins? No. He called to say he'd be by later today. I assume it's to tell me about Terry's will. I'm going to inherit this house."

CHAPTER 22

Ellen Garvey was our next stop. Joshua Collins was just leaving. "We meet again," he said as he passed by.

I assumed he'd started with the new beneficiary first. The easier of his visits? I wasn't sure.

"I hope you got the information you needed from Carol and Martin," she said as soon as we were back in her living room. "I asked them to be thorough."

"Yes, thank you for alerting them in advance. One of my staff is reviewing both sets of documents," Herc told her.

After being seated, she gave us an expectant look. Apparently she was prepared to answer further questions, but she wasn't volunteering anything.

"We noted that Terry Seiser's attorney, Joshua Collins, was just here," he began. "Could you tell us the reason for his visit?"

"I thought you already knew," she replied. "Apparently I was named a beneficiary in Terry's will."

"The beneficiary," Herc said pointedly. "Did you know about that?"

"No! This is a total surprise. Terry never mentioned he'd named me."

"How do you account for his decision?" I asked.

"Frankly, I can't."

"But you were seeing him socially, weren't you, besides working with him on the marathon?" I asked.

"Yes, but it wasn't all that serious. At least it wasn't with me." She didn't look away. She stared at me straight on. "Like I told you before, he wasn't an easy man to get to know. I was intrigued that he was interested in me, so I went along with him."

"Did you plan to see him after the marathon?" I asked.

She tilted her head to the side. "I don't know. I hadn't thought about it."

"Did you see him in your future?" Herc asked.

"Why are you asking me these questions? Any relationship I had with him ended with his death. I don't mean to sound harsh, but that's how I feel."

"Were you aware he'd only recently changed his will when he named you beneficiary?" I asked.

"No, of course not. I told you, being named beneficiary is news to me. He never told me that was his plan."

"He'd previously named his housekeeper and business manager at the hardware store as his beneficiaries," Herc went on. "Now they're out."

She blinked, like he'd struck her. "I, uh, didn't know that. Do they know yet?"

"They will soon if they are still unaware," Herc replied.

She folded her hands in her lap and let one thumb rub the other. "I'm sorry. They must be devastated."

"We can't speak to that yet," I replied.

"I don't know what to say. I met each of them once or twice when I was with Terry. He treated them shabbily, and yes, I was aware how he could be to other people. I got the feeling each of them would have left him years ago but for some power he held over them."

She'd picked up on the situation with Muriel Fox. But I was surprised to hear what she said about Carmen Loomis. "Did you call him on it?" I asked.

"No, even I didn't feel comfortable getting that personal with him." She thought some more about her reply. "Wait, he did say something about his housekeeper when I was there once, and I commented on the exchange I'd observed. Just a few weeks ago, now that I think back on it. She'd quizzed him about what time he'd be getting home that evening. On the face of it, she could have simply been ascertaining if she needed to keep his dinner warm for him or even if he wanted dinner. But it struck me how her tone sounded more like that of a wife."

"Could you expand on that?" Herc asked.

"Not very easily. It was more of an impression. It was like she was trying to guilt him into coming home early for once, as if she had every right to expect such. She looked at me like I was the enemy, luring him away at night."

She did a good job describing what she'd meant. I could picture a look like that.

"While we were still there and she was out of earshot, I asked him if he realized she was in love with him. He laughed it off, saying she stuck around because she didn't have the skills to do anything else. As long as he could get someone to work for him at the pittance he paid her, he wasn't about to rock the boat with a romance. He said, 'And besides, look at her. How could anyone love that sad sack?'"

Wow. I knew Terry Seiser was a scumbag, but what she'd just related about his comment was a new low. "How did you react to his words?" I asked.

"Not well, although I didn't say anything more at the time. I didn't want to risk losing his participation in the marathon that close to the event."

Herc and I remained silent. She appeared to realize how she herself had come off. "I guess that answers your question about my future plans with him. Which makes the fact that he named me in his will even more uncomfortable. I asked Collins if there was some way I could refuse the estate, and he said yes but not to decide right then. But I swear I didn't know those two women had received nothing."

We didn't reply.

"Wait! Do you think I killed him for his money?" Her voice rose several notes.

"Did you?" Herc asked.

"No!" She ran both hands through her hair. "This is crazy. What started out to bring the community together and at the same time raise funds for low-income housing has turned upside down. Everyone suspects everyone else of killing him, and two good women have been cheated out of what should have been coming to them."

Again, not much we could say, but Herc tried. "The sooner we can identify the murderer, the sooner things can return to normal. Maybe not the normal you planned, but something beyond the weekend's disaster."

"I guess I understand, Lieutenant Morgan. You have your job to do. I'm sorry this all came to pass, that's all."

On that note, we got out of there immediately.

"What did you make of her denials?" I asked Herc.

He didn't reply until the car was underway. "Although perhaps a little more melodramatic than I expected or was necessary, I believe her. Why Seiser named her in his will totally escapes me other than it was his way of hurting the people who'd been most loyal to him."

"We haven't even discussed his skipping over his cousin, Al. Should we get his take on this?"

Herc glanced at his watch. "The day is slipping away from us, and as much information as we've gathered, I still don't see a clear suspect. Just possible contenders. As much as I'm loath to check back with Fox and Loomis, we need to catch them now while their feelings from being left out of the will are raw."

"You're right," I said ruefully. "We won't be well received."

"Are we ever?"

"I'm trying to maintain an open mind, Herc, but I really hate what that guy did to those two women."

"I don't disagree, but we've been down this path before. Just watch and listen carefully. This is when they're most vulnerable and most apt to reveal their real feelings."

Muriel Fox took even longer to come to the door of the hardware store. "Don't you have anyone else to harass?" she asked. "I've told you and told you again everything I know about Terry and the store's finances."

"Just a couple questions this time," Herc said, ignoring her opening comment. "We assume you've now heard from Seiser's attorney, Joshua Collins. Did you know you'd been left out of his will?"

She didn't even take us to her office this time. She stood, hands on hips in the main part of the store, but she did take a step back. "Good news travels fast, huh? No, I'd been led to believe by Terry that the store and all the inventory were coming to me. I don't know if I'd have been working so hard since Saturday if I'd been aware it was all for naught. I understand that woman he's been palling around with, that Garvey woman, gets everything. Like she needs it."

"How do you feel about that?" I asked. Stupid question, but we had to take advantage of her current state of shock.

"I just told you. There's nothing here for me anymore. I'll have to find an attorney I can ill afford to learn whether I must deal with the IRS. If I do, you can be sure I will tell them as much as I know about his playing with the books."

"That's what he's held over you, isn't it?" Herc said.

She licked her lips, her eyes fearful. "You found out about that? What are you going to do about it?"

"If you didn't kill him, nothing," Herc replied. "If you do turn out to be our killer, we've got your motive. You couldn't let Seiser continue to hold this over you and force you to falsify the records."

"I didn't kill him."

"Besides eliminating your antagonist, you thought you'd be inheriting the store. With Seiser out of the way, you could've put the business back on its feet legally. Those are two pretty solid reasons for getting rid of the man."

Tears streamed down her face. "I'm a God-fearing woman. I would've killed him long ago if that was in me, but it's not."

"Thank you for answering our questions," I said, trying not to sympathize too much. "If anything more occurs to you or if you want to tell us more, you know how to contact us."

Back in the car, neither of us spoke almost the entire way to Seiser's house. "That wasn't easy, I know," Herc said at last. "And this next one won't be any easier. We uncovered two good motives back there with Fox. She broke down, but she held her ground about not killing him."

Carmen Loomis held her ground as well. "No, I had no idea Terry changed his mind about leaving me the house until Mr. Collins showed up not long ago. Terry could be cruel at times, but I never suspected he could tell me one thing and do another."

"That gives you a pretty good motive for killing him then," Herc said. "You were tired of being taken for granted, for his lack of appreciation of your loyalty, so you did him in for the money."

"No, I didn't kill him," she said. "I might've received the house in his will, but there wouldn't have been any other money coming in if he was no longer around to run the hardware store and lumberyard."

"What will you do now that you didn't receive the house?" I asked.

She shrugged. "I don't know. This horrible turn of events is too new. I have to think it through. Maybe Ms. Garvey will take pity on me, consider me a low-income project, and let me stay here."

Good luck with that, but given what Garvey had said just recently, maybe it wasn't too far out of the question.

"Is that all, now that you've come here to gloat at my change of fortune?" she asked.

"That wasn't our intent, Mrs. Loomis," Herc told her, for once replying to a comment.

Nonetheless, we got out of there as soon as we could.

Had we just spoken with the murderer, or was our culprit still out there?

CHAPTER 23

Our work day wasn't over yet. It was time to return to the white boards at my duplex, but first we decided to stop off and see how Al was doing.

"Have you come to tell me you've got my cousin's murderer in jail?" he asked when he opened the door.

"You know better than that, partner," Herc said, edging his way into the room. The coffee table was littered with fast-food bags and wrappers and beer cans. The usually fastidious Aloysius Buford was taking his cousin's death hard. "Ro and I are making good progress, but Seiser had a slew of enemies and people he treated poorly. It's been challenging to weed out the complainers from those with a real ax to grind."

Al slumped into an easy chair after first removing an abandoned tee-shirt from it. "Yeah, I get it. It's just that I haven't had much more to do the last few days other than decide on arrangements at the funeral home. I want to be out in the field working by your side, although I know that's not the best idea."

"I've never been in your position," Herc said, "but I'm sure sitting on the sidelines can't be easy."

"I'm waiting for the medical examiner to release his body. He's pretty much completed his review of Terry's injuries, and the upshot is still the same as his original finding: Terry was struck on the head with a blunt object. That didn't kill him. It just made it possible for his killer to drag his body under the viewing stand. He died from numerous bodily injuries caused by both the impact and then the pressure of the collapsed structure."

"Did he indicate how soon he'll be able to release the body?" I asked. Herc and I had just been exchanging texts with Kelsey on his progress.

"He and the forensics team haven't established exactly how the collapse occurred. The obvious answer is that parties unknown, the killer, caused it to fall. But the how part is the question. He's holding onto the body on the outside chance that further review of the injuries could lead to that answer."

This man needed closure, and for the time being it was suspended. Possibly by Herc and me because we'd been focusing on the suspects and not the collapse itself. I hoped Val had had a chance to study the design plan I'd given her.

I searched my brain for something to occupy his mind. "How about a memorial service? Are you planning one?" I asked.

"Thought about it, like it was the thing to do. But the more I considered the idea, the less sense it made. Memorial services are for the living, the survivors. In Terry's case, who would come? Maybe his housekeeper and his business manager because they'd think they owed it to him, but I doubt anyone else would show. Terry wasn't liked. Surely that's come through in all the interviews you've conducted."

"Uh, Al?" Herc said.

"Yeah?"

"What do you know about your cousin's will?"

Al sat back, steepled his fingers and leaned them against his chin. "That's your sensitive way of asking if I knew I wasn't inheriting anything from him?"

At least we wouldn't have to be the bearers of that good news.

"Uh, yeah. We talked to Joshua Collins, his attorney, earlier. Apparently your cousin had intended to leave the business to his business manager and his home to his housekeeper until recently, when he changed his mind and left everything to his, uh, to Ellen Garvey."

"Don't worry, you guys. I've known for some time I wouldn't be inheriting. The subject came up during one of the rare dinners we shared. He asked me what I wanted. Threw me. We were both reasonably young still, though both of us unattached. At the time, it seemed like such a far-off prospect, I didn't pay much attention to his question other than to ask if he was sick or something. After he reassured me he was in good shape, I told him I didn't really want anything. What would I do with that business? Or even his house? I'm happy with my current circumstances."

"You could've sold both of them," Herc said.

"And done what with the proceeds? Like I said, I like my life just the way it is. Okay, a full-time job in Orlando doing forensic accounting wouldn't be bad, but no amount of money will bring me that."

Although he didn't realize it, Al had just risen considerably in my estimation. Until now I'd dismissed him as the prissy, by-the-book follow-up partner to Herc after his memorable days with me. But his loyalty to his cousin, despite the man's personality, was commendable. Now we were learning he'd turned down the possible chance of additional riches.

"Did you know he had named Ellen Garvey as his sole beneficiary?" I asked.

Al shook his head. "No. If he'd asked me what I thought about that plan, I would've advised against it. But I had no idea things had gotten so close between the two of them that he'd leave all his worldly goods to her. Not that there's anything wrong with her, although I hardly know her. But those who'd worked for him all these years should've been recognized in some way."

"Apparently his decision was a surprise all around," Herc said.

Al nodded. "That's the way he was. Must've been torqued off by either his housekeeper or his business manager or both. Probably would've changed things back once he got over whatever had miffed him. Thought he had many more years to live. You don't think his will was the killer's motive, do you?"

"That's why we're here," Herc replied. "We didn't know him, but you did. Would he have held the possibility of inheriting from him over anyone as revenge or incentive or something we haven't even thought of?"

"The business is in poor shape, as I'm sure you've already discovered. His house is okay but not that valuable. I'm not sure anyone would want them. You probably thought I was so noble turning them down, but I saw them more as albatrosses I didn't need around my neck."

My estimate of him, which had so recently improved, now changed again. Al wasn't so honorable as realistic. Even better.

Herc's shoulders had collapsed along with the curve of his mouth. "What's the matter, man?" Al asked.

"We thought we'd hit on the motive for his murder. Either his housekeeper or his business manager or even the lumberyard guy might've had hopes of improving their lives by inheriting. You've upset that apple cart."

"I said they didn't mean much to me, but that's not to say one or more of them didn't see it that way."

"While we're on the subject of motives, any other idea?" I asked Al. He'd been sitting around here in his apartment the last few days. Surely he'd been thinking about such things.

"Revenge?" he said at length. "He could be a real stinker. Perhaps someone couldn't take it any longer?"

"Which still covers those three parties," I said. "Or jealousy?"

"Jealousy?" Al replied. "Hadn't thought of that. Who'd be jealous of him?"

"He and Ellen Garvey appeared to be getting closer than others liked. Others such as her financial advisor and the marathon consultant," I said.

"How about Ellen Garvey herself," Al asked, "since she's the one who's benefited the most from Terry's death?"

"To the best of our knowledge, she didn't know about the bequest," I said. "But more than that consideration, why would she do something so destructive to her event? Unless there was some concern about proceeding with the marathon that we have yet to learn about?"

"Would their insurance cover a budget overage?" Al said.

"We hadn't considered that reason yet," Herc replied. "But none of the committee, particularly Martin Brockhurst, the accounting guy, have seemed alarmed at that prospect."

Now we were just spinning our wheels to let Al feel like he was participating in the investigation. Herc must have sensed it, too, because he next said we had one more stop yet this day. We left Al, asking him to let us know if he thought of anything more about his cousin.

As for us, it was time to check in with Val.

CHAPTER 24

t was after five when we left Al's. Val had texted me fifteen minutes prior saying she'd gone home for the day and was ready to discuss the design plan.

"How do you think he's doing?" I asked as we drove toward my duplex.

"Al? His frustrations are coming at him from more than one direction," Herc said thoughtfully. "He's grieving for his cousin, even though he says they weren't all that close, and all the responsibility for putting the guy to rest has fallen on him. He's also enraged that someone had the gall to murder Seiser." His right index and middle fingers drummed the steering wheel. "But as much as the death and the murder are on his mind, it's really getting to him that he's sidelined. Voluntarily, but that's eating away at him just the same."

"And not that I'm the one who *gets* to investigate?" I asked.

"No, not at all. Don't forget he *asked* you to come on board."

"Thanks for reminding me. Now it's up to the two of us to reassure him he made the right decision."

Val was waiting for us in my kitchen when we got to my half of the duplex. "I was starting to think you didn't care what I thought about this design plan," she said as I poured water for both Herc and me. Though I would've preferred wine, I needed to keep a clear head as we reviewed the day's findings.

"We stopped by Al's to see how he's doing," Herc said, after having taken a large gulp of the liquid. "Didn't feel we could leave until he'd had his say."

"Not to worry. Jim's at some community committee meeting and isn't due home for another hour. I've already greeted our feline landlord and given him his dinner. I can't believe you left him alone with that tree all day. It looks great, by the way. Must've been Chuck's idea."

"I like Christmas trees, too," I replied, not taking offense. "Chuck's just more into them. We gave Jason all day yesterday to get used to his space being invaded and to assure ourselves he wouldn't attack it in our absence."

"He got to some of the balls," she said, reminding me of an older child reporting the sins of the younger sibling.

"Those are from the pet store made specifically for the purpose of keeping pets entertained and away from the main event. Chuck had heard such a thing existed and went out last night to find them."

She set aside her glass of wine and pulled out the design plan. "Let's get down to business. You've already had a long day."

Herc grabbed a kitchen chair across the table from her. "What's your take on that viewing stand?"

She replied with her own question. "Who did you say designed the platform?"

"I didn't. All we have is that sketchy signature on the cover page. We haven't been able to find anyone by that name in either the architectural or engineering organizations," I replied. "Why do you ask?"

"On the surface, the plan appears to be legit. The structure should've held up. It's just that I've never seen a plan quite like this. It's like it was written in a foreign language. At least by someone unfamiliar with standard design layout."

"That was my take on it as well," I said. "But I needed you to verify that."

"Were you aware the structure was designed to be temporary?" she asked.

"We'd heard as much," Herc said. "So that it could be reused at other marathons and outdoor events."

She nodded in agreement. "Okay, I get that. It appears each corner is joined by one bolt, which if loosened could cause the frame to slip, but that alone shouldn't have brought the rest down."

I studied the design plan with new eyes and tried to envision the action she'd described. I'd noticed those corner bolts earlier but hadn't truly realized what could've happened simply with strategic twists. "What else had to happen?"

"That's hard to say. If the structure had been built to plan, the rest should've remained intact, although maybe a little wobbly. It's possible something like a rope was attached to the outside floor somewhere. When pulled, it could've brought down the entire structure. But it would've taken considerable force. Were there no security cameras in place to record the incident?"

"Not directly focused on that spot," Herc replied. "Yeah, I know. There shoulda been. Hindsight and all that."

"Were any photos taken of the structure once it was completed?" she asked.

Herc pulled them up on his computer and showed her. "Just these. The screen wasn't removed until two days before the event. Ellen Garvey, the woman who oversaw the marathon, wouldn't let the victim, Seiser, who built it, put it off any longer, because she needed to promote the structure on social media. But he limited her to only taking these."

"And no one else besides Ellen and the committee was allowed anywhere near that part of the park," I added.

She gazed at the screen for well over a minute, scrolling back and forth amongst the four photos. "When was construction completed?"

"Good question. We haven't been able to establish the exact time it was finished. Seiser apparently was very cagey about the platform's status. It may not even have been done when the others got to see it," I said.

Val yanked her head back like a parakeet eyeing a cat staring through its cage. "I don't get it. Was he doing something illegal? Or attempting to do it all himself?"

A theory had been developing in my head. "I can only guess what was going on with him, since he didn't share his plans with Ellen Garvey or anyone else on the planning committee and certainly not the people at the hardware store and lumberyard."

"What do you think he was up to, Ro?" Herc asked.

"Given what we've learned about the man's personality, my guess is that after he'd made such a play to take over the project, he discovered he was in over his head. But Seiser's ego wouldn't let him ask for help, so he cloaked the whole project in secrecy."

"I agree," Herc replied, "but what was he doing behind that curtain?"

I continued with my hypothesis. "He apparently was the one who demanded the structure be easily disassembled. That makes a certain amount of sense now, because the idea of being able to recycle the platform for other events relates well to the current attention to sustainability. I think he got lucky on that one. Someone on the committee or otherwise involved in the community could have made a pitch to make it a permanent fixture of the park, which wouldn't require the extra expense of storing it or taking it down and reassembling it from year to year. But apparently no one did."

Herc screwed up his eyes, taking in my idea. "How would making it easy to tear down have contributed to his keeping secret his inability to pull off the plan?"

"This is still all speculation. We already know he'd backed off his original offer to contribute the materials and was recouping his costs by charging the event committee. Supposing he thought he could get away with storing the components and charging whoever needed them for future events. If his actions were ever questioned, maybe he thought he could pass off the cost of maintaining the structure from year to year as the cost of doing business."

"If we hadn't discovered how preposterous his role on the committee and his relationship with Ellen Garvey was, I'd say you were out of your mind," Herc said.

Val had remained quiet throughout my discourse. Now she spoke up. "What you've just described, Mom, reminds me of a plot from one of those movie thrillers. Was this Seiser guy that smart?"

Herc answered for me. "Smart? No, or he wouldn't have let his business go downhill. But your mom hit on a key to this whole tragedy by referring to his ego. As the realization of his dilemma dawned on him, he could've admitted as much to Ellen Garvey. She would've probably asked him what additional help he needed or offered to reassign him to another facet of the committee that would've given him the same amount of visibility but less stress. But he didn't. Instead, he kept digging his hole deeper."

"But he didn't dig an actual hole," Val said. "Which would have been the smart thing to do to keep the framework secure." She continued to study the photos. "Those look like tire tracks on that one section of the ground. That makes sense. He would have had to have all the materials brought in. He couldn't carry them."

Her words resonated in my brain. "That's right, Val! He couldn't carry in everything by himself. We'd been thinking he drove his materials right up to the structure in his pickup. But even then, he still couldn't manage everything. Cyrus Milligan, the marathon consultant, told us Seiser hired a small crew, which is probably why he insisted on the screen. He wanted to maintain the perception that he built the platform on his own."

Herc set his glass of water down so hard, some of the liquid spilled onto the table. "Ro! That is brilliant!"

"Hey! I'm the one that put her onto that idea," Val said, offering a fake pout.

"Thank you, my child," I said, patting her back. "I can't believe we hadn't already thought of that method, but now that we have, you've given us new directions to explore tomorrow."

CHAPTER 25

Chuck arrived home just after Val left. "Solve the case yet?" he asked ever so hopefully.

"Getting there," Herc replied.

Chuck set his bag of to-go boxes from the restaurant on the table. "Christmas is four days off, you guys. Please tell me you'll take the full day off, Ro, if you haven't wrapped it by then."

"But no pressure, right?" I returned kiddingly, taking a moment to exchange a hug and a brief kiss.

"Well … Anything I can do to help?" he asked.

"Can you keep dinner warm while Herc and I summarize the day's findings? Then, barring any unforeseen clues popping in on us, I'm free to enjoy the rest of the evening with you."

"Deal!" he said. "Just let me check out the condition of our tree and I'll leave the dining room free to the two of you. Want to stay for lasagna, Herc? I brought home plenty."

Who was this man? I couldn't remember a time when he'd extended a dinner invite to my partner, not that Herc hadn't invited himself on occasion.

"Thanks, but I've got other plans tonight," Herc replied. "Luann has signed us up for caroling with a group from the fire department."

"Caroling? You?" I asked, surprised.

"What can I say? She's got me participating in more holiday festivities than I ever knew existed. I drew the line at wearing a holiday sweater."

Chuck was pleased that his holiday balls for cats seemed to be doing their job, although with Herc in the house, Jason had long ago disappeared. Having determined the living and dining rooms were still in good shape, Chuck returned to the kitchen.

"I can't believe we've only been on this case two full days," I said as I approached the white boards. "My brain is stuffed with so many different details. I hope this exercise helps us zero in on the most critical."

We started by enumerating what we'd learned about Terry Seiser.

1. *Businesses failing. Didn't understand how to manage. Seemed more interested in using the businesses' assets for his own needs.*
2. *Not liked by most.*
3. *Appears to have taken advantage of his business manager, Muriel Fox, and housekeeper, Carmen Loomis.*
4. *Divorced years ago. Former wife left him, died about 5 years ago.*
5. *Despite his negative personality, seemed to consider himself a ladies' man. Most recent flame Ellen Garvey.*
6. *Garvey put him on her marathon planning committee, even though he had no background in running or planning events.*
7. *Though it wasn't his idea, he convinced Garvey to put him in charge of building a viewing stand along the end of the route. He originally offered to provide the materials free of charge but switched that to expecting the committee to foot the bill.*
8. *Very secretive about the construction. Wouldn't let anyone help him or even observe his progress. Put up a screen around the structure. Hypothesis: didn't want to admit he didn't know what he was doing. Probably hired a crew to help him.*

9. *Changed his will recently, removing business manager and housekeeper as beneficiaries and naming Ellen Garvey as sole beneficiary.*

MURIEL FOX — BUSINESS MANAGER

1. *Has worked for Seiser ever since high school. Started out mainly as bookkeeper but duties expanded over time, especially after Bill Seiser died, to the point where she is the main one to handle all the business details. Seiser liked to think he was the public relations guy, although given his personality, that didn't quite come off.*
2. *Concerned about pending visit from IRS because Seiser had been loose with the books.*
3. *Seiser was holding something over her head to keep her around.*
4. *What she'll do now that she was left out of will remains to be seen.*

CARMEN LOOMIS — HOUSEKEEPER

1. *Came to work for Seiser after husband killed in work accident years ago. Recommended to Seiser by Al Buford.*
2. *Seems to take great pride in the way she runs the house. She's the only staff he has.*
3. *Lives in her own suite on premises.*
4. *Appearance changed from Saturday to Monday, when she wore makeup.*
5. *Appeared loyal to Seiser but not necessarily fond of him.*
6. *Like Fox, recently struck from will. Unknown what she will do now.*

Gordo Zaharian — manager of lumberyard

1. *Worked for Bill Seiser as assistant lumberyard manager. Made manager by Joshua Collins when prior manager retired.*
2. *No love lost between him and Terry Seiser. Accused Seiser of living off the profits coming in from the lumberyard to the point where lumberyard also going downhill as well.*
3. *He and Fox run the two businesses separately, although the revenue from the lumberyard flows into the hardware store.*

Before moving on to the marathon committee, we backed up and considered both Shane Bolton and Al.

Shane Bolton — manager of The Sandpiper

1. *Worked for the older Seiser when younger. Outshone Terry in his job performance, which didn't endear him to the younger man. Left the hardware store before Bill Seiser passed away.*
2. *Only ran into Terry recently when they both wound up on the marathon committee, although Shane was mainly concerned with the Reindeer Run Rendezvous.*
3. *The two had words the night of the Rendezvous. Had to be broken up by Daryl Henson, security guy.*
4. *No alibi for early Saturday morning when Seiser was killed.*

Al Buford — Seiser's cousin

1. *Asked us to handle the investigation since he was too close.*
2. *Didn't see his cousin often but he was Seiser's only relative.*
3. *Knew he wasn't in the will but had earlier told Seiser he didn't want the business or his house.*

The marathon committee

ELLEN GARVEY — PHILANTHROPIST AND SEISER'S RECENT GIRLFRIEND

1. *Inherited millions from her businessman husband, Neils, who made his fortune converting old mom-and-pop filling stations to modern convenience stores. She was formerly a fourth-grade teacher.*
2. *Met Seiser about 6 months ago, only recently started going out with him.*
3. *Already working with Carol McGiver on some type of event near the end of the year to raise funds and awareness of Project Phoenix for low-income housing.*
4. *Brought Seiser onto the planning committee last fall. At his insistence, put him in charge of constructing the viewing platform.*
5. *Agreed to absorb platform building expenses when Seiser backed out of his original offer to donate the materials.*
6. *Seiser recently named her his only beneficiary to her surprise.*

CAROL MCGIVER — HEAD OF PROJECT PHOENIX BUILDING HOMES FOR LOWER INCOME FAMILIES

1. *Met Ellen Garvey when she rescued her from a broken-down bike several months ago.*
2. *They struck up an immediate friendship, with Garvey wanting to do something to help the project grow.*
3. *Carol has served as the information chair on the committee.*

MARTIN BROCKHURST — GARVEY'S FINANCIAL ADVISOR

1. *Garvey's third financial advisor after the first two couldn't handle the job.*
2. *Over the past three years has helped her build even greater revenues through his wise investment advice.*

3. *Not the greatest supporter of her philanthropic efforts because he didn't want to see all his investment efforts go for naught.*

4. *Suggested the idea of a marathon because his brother, Wally, is a runner.*

Cyrus Milligan — Marathon Consultant

1. *Brought on board when it quickly became clear Wally Brockhurst wasn't that knowledgeable, although Milligan's credits are somewhat sketchy as well.*

2. *Even with his credentials, he hasn't been that helpful in some respects. For instance, he didn't advise a security camera, nor did he strongly endorse a budget be established early on and adhered to.*

3. *He seems to have resented how Seiser moved in on Garvey.*

4. *He supplied the design plan.*

I glanced up at Herc as I finished writing that last line. "Anything immediately come to mind that I missed? I just let the info flow. Let's think about it overnight and review it tomorrow."

"Only thing I'd add is to list who else we should still talk to," he said.

"Now that we've received Val's input about the design plan, we should pin down Milligan as to who he actually got the plan from," I said.

"And we should check back with Oliver. See what more background info she's uncovered on the lot of them," Herc added.

He made ready to leave. "That lasagna sounded pretty good, but I've gotta go home and vocalize before I start decking the halls."

I raised a brow. "Did you just say *vocalize?*"

"Yeah, I did. But don't mention it again."

"Too bad. You've just given me the greatest of blackmail tools. Go enjoy yourself tonight. Tomorrow we start again."

CHAPTER 26

"Can you picture it? Herc being part of a caroling group?" I asked Chuck over our lasagna.

His fork rested midair while he contemplated my question. "Not really, but I can see him faking it while he's standing next to Luann Corey giving the performance of his life. He really seems to have found someone special. I'm truly happy for him. Not just because he seems to have backed away from his jealousy of me, but because he's basically one of the good guys and deserves to be as happy as I am."

I set down my fork, momentarily ignoring the deliciousness I was about to consume. "That's very high-minded of you."

His eyes seemed to arrest mine. "Maybe. But did you hear that last part? I'm a happy guy these days. And that's not because I'm delighted my businesses are doing well." He shot a glance at Jason, who'd settled in his favorite corner of the kitchen, licking his paws, appearing every bit disinterested in our conversation but hanging on every word. "Nor because I'm happy you and I are getting along these days, my fine friend." Back to me. "No, despite my best efforts to maintain a sensible distance from you, Rowena Summerfield, I'm crazy about you. Sharing the holidays with you is making me even more aware of my feelings."

How had I been so lucky to have this caring, understanding … gorgeous … man come into my life? He seemed to be enjoying the holidays despite my involvement in the Seiser case. I reached for his hand. "Your willingness to put your feelings right out there takes my breath away. It humbles me. I hope you know they are reciprocated, even though I'm not very good at it thanks to years of hiding my emotions behind my badge."

"I'd say you're doing just fine."

We sat like that for what seemed hours although it was just seconds. At some point during that moment, Jason left the room. Too much sentimentality for him. Or more to the point, no one was concentrating on him.

Chuck was the first to snap out of it. "As pleasant as this has been, basking in each other's presence, we should decide what to do this evening. What more can we do to celebrate the holidays tonight?"

"Cuddle up on the sofa and drink hot chocolate?" I spoke.

"Nice suggestion, but we could do that almost any night. Don't you want to go out and be part of everyone else's cele-brations?"

No. I'd been on the go all day. But I was discovering my man was seriously into this holiday thing. If Herc could don a muffler and pretend-sing, I could drum up some enthusiasm for some other festivity. "Okay, got any ideas?" I asked, laying it on him. I'd already done my part with the hot chocolate thing.

He returned to his lasagna. "Actually, I do. One of my wine suppliers is providing the mulled wine for the dessert and beverage stand at the end of the tour of holiday lights tonight. All you have to do is bring a sweater for the car."

Floridians might not have snow for Christmas, but we had the advantage of good weather. That allowed us to do more outdoors than might be possible in the more northern climes. Home lighting competitions came to the top of the list. I hadn't really paid much attention to them over the years, focusing my design interest and energies on the interior of homes rather than the exterior.

Tickets weren't required for this event, but it helped to have a list of addresses and a map of the town in advance rather than just driving around looking for the lights. We stopped at a kiosk downtown to pick them up. We also received a ballot to vote for Best in Show.

The idea was to follow the other vehicles on the route, remaining in the vehicle most of the way, but two neighborhoods made that nearly impossible for the viewers. Every house was not only brilliantly lit but had added mechanical toys and other holiday features. Parking lots in nearby fields had been established for viewers to take in the decorations up close.

Apparently a competition between the two neighborhoods had developed over the years, because homeowners were openly standing in front of their residences vying for votes. Some were even giving away candy canes or other holiday goodies. Chuck took it upon himself to accept two candy canes. "Now Christmas is really official," he said, presenting one to me.

I'm not much for hard candy. I'm more a milk chocolate fan myself. But tonight as we enjoyed the holiday together, it was the sweetest treat I'd enjoyed in a long time.

"Have you done this before?" I asked when we were back in the car.

"Truthfully, never." He squeezed my hand. "I've known about the lights. Who can avoid them this time of year? More and more homeowners have been participating in recent years. But I never cared all that much about enjoying them before."

"Same here, but I'm glad you suggested we do this tonight," I replied. "Thanks for pushing for us to do more holiday-type stuff this year. I haven't gotten so involved since Val was younger and Ben was alive."

We drove a block or two before either of us spoke.

"That's the first time you've been able to mention your late husband without hesitating before you completed the sentence. Is that indicative of anything?"

I considered the idea. I hadn't brought up Ben in a long time, not that I'd forgotten him by any means.

Chuck was waiting for an answer.

"I don't know. I didn't realize that was the case when I just spoke. Years ago, when I first was widowed, others told me I'd reach this point someday. I couldn't set it at a specific date. I would just realize that I'd moved on without leaving him behind. Perhaps that is the case now. If I have, that's in large part thanks to you."

"I appreciate the thought, but I can't take all the credit. You had to be ready to consider a new life. I just gave you a little nudge."

"Ben was sick for several months. During that time, we talked about the life that lay ahead for me and Val. In a way, despite the horror of his death, we were lucky, because we had a chance to prepare for those changes, unlike people who experience a sudden death. Anyway, he told me if I ever found someone else, I shouldn't feel I was cheating on him. Instead, I should embrace new love openly and be happy."

"Wise man. I'm sorry I didn't know him," Chuck said.

"You would've liked each other." I meant it and suddenly realized I'd internalized my late husband's spirit and he was there for me as I moved on.

I sensed Chuck had more to say, but at that point we approached the second neighborhood group project, and we spent the next few minutes oohing and aahing and pointing out features we hadn't seen in the first neighborhood.

Early in my career, I'd done a stint in traffic control. I'd never lost my appreciation of moving many vehicles through a narrow space quickly and safely, so as awe-inspiring as the lights and decorations were, I was more impressed with how easy it was for Chuck to maneuver his way through the queue of cars. He, of course, was under the impression our viewing ease had been made possible by his better-than-average driving skills, which weren't bad. But I knew that a traffic engineer or team somewhere had designed the route that was enhancing our viewing pleasure. No need to inform him otherwise.

Within minutes of departing the neighborhood display, we arrived at the end of the course. Chuck pulled into a parking lot, turned off the car and leaned over to me. "Ready for that mulled wine I promised?"

Not really. I liked my wine white and chilled, not red and warmed with spices. But Chuck apparently had been anticipating this stop more than I'd realized. "I thought we'd never get here," I lied, figuring a white lie was better than bursting his balloon.

I'd pictured joining other Christmas lighting enthusiasts in a party tent. Instead, Chuck led me into a downtown bar that had been taken over for the event. Twinkle lights had replaced the usual neon lighting for the night. The bar was covered in red and white checked tablecloths. Christmas songs played in the background.

Without the least bit of hesitation, I slipped into the Christmas spirit. Chuck had been doing everything in his power to get me here, but this bar hit the nail on the head, especially after my first sip of mulled wine.

Chuck hovered over me like a parent watching his child take its first step after he handed me my mug. Anxious and simultaneously excited. "Do you like it?"

I took a few seconds more to savor the taste of cherries, grapes and cinnamon on my tongue before responding. "Delicious!" This time I wasn't lying.

Jason couldn't have purred louder if he'd been there. "There's chocolate-peppermint brownies and chocolate cheesecake, if you want."

"Wow, we've hit the mother lode, but I'll have to decline those. You go ahead, though."

"Nah, I was asking to be polite. Are you ready to leave?"

I placed my empty mug back on the bar top and let Chuck escort me out of the building. "That was a truly unique experience. This whole evening has been. Thanks, Chuck. I appreciate the way you've been putting yourself out to get me into the spirit even more than the experiences themselves."

He leaned over and kissed my cheek. "You don't know how much I've been waiting to hear those words." He paused, as if debating whether to add something. "There's just one more thing that would top off the night for me. Are you up for it?"

How should I reply to such a broad-based question? "Uh, sure."

He took my hand and led me down the street past two more businesses until he abruptly stopped before another. A jewelry store.

He gazed at me shyly. "There's a question I want to ask you, Ro. When we talked about your late husband earlier tonight, I got the impression you were ready to move on. Does that mean you'd be willing to hear what I have to ask?"

Oh, no! Not tonight. I wasn't ready to hear this yet, was I? My throat had gone dry. I couldn't have answered him now, even if I knew what I'd be saying.

He leaned down and kissed the top of my head. "Scared you, didn't I? Obviously you weren't expecting me to go quite so far tonight. In truth, I hadn't planned this until we got to talking earlier." He took my hand in his. "I didn't mean to ambush you. I was just gauging what kind of reaction I'd get if I gave you a ring for Christmas."

Fortunately, my voice returned in time to say something, even if it wasn't the response he wanted to hear. "Oh, Chuck. I just realized tonight that I was ready to consider committing to someone besides Ben. The feeling is so new, I need a little time to get used to it. Could you hold onto that question just a little longer?"

I saw disappointment in his eyes, but in a flash, it morphed into hope. "You are worth waiting for, Rowena Summerfield. But I must warn you, all this Christmas spirit of love and family is working on me. I can't guarantee I can remain patient much longer."

I didn't dare tell him how close I was to answering his question. Instead, I covered my temptation with a hearty kiss.

CHAPTER 27

Neither Herc nor I were especially chipper the next morning as we stopped off first for coffee. Normally, one of us would have brought in doughnuts or other goodies, but today Herc suggested stopping at our favorite coffee shop before meeting up with Janet Oliver for her report.

"How was caroling last night?" I asked once we'd both taken a few sips of the precious brew.

He stared back at me with red eyes. "Apparently one gets pretty thirsty after singing outside for over an hour. This bar downtown was serving something it called wassail to anyone who participated in the holiday lights tour. Our group was invited since we performed on one of the corners along the route. No one warned me how much alcohol was in the stuff."

"Chuck and I were at that same bar after we took the tour. I'm surprised we didn't see you. And didn't you taste the wine in that stuff?"

"You took in the lights?" he asked incredulously.

"Yes? Why do you sound so surprised?"

He shrugged. "Doesn't sound like you, that's all."

"I take in community events on occasion. Didn't I just help Shane Bolton with the Reindeer Run Rendezvous?"

He eyed me like he was about to challenge my statement. "You didn't see our group when you drove by? We were on the corner near that fancy home where that performance artist lives."

"Luke Jarvis? No, I guess I was too busy taking in his lighting display. Looked like all three artists in the house applied their creativity to the exterior. I wouldn't be surprised if they won grand prize, unless they're disqualified because they're professionals."

"Okay, I told you why I'm under the weather this morning. How 'bout you? No red eyes, like me, but you've been uncharacteristically quiet. Don't tell me you and Deli Man had words?"

Leave it to his detective instincts to kick in now. He was right. My mind had been elsewhere ever since Chuck brought up "the question" when we were in front of the jewelry store. Chuck had wisely not pushed me to say anything more than I had.

I hadn't slept well, and my mood carried over to this morning. Time to snap out of it. We had a murder to solve. "Everything's fine between Chuck and me. But you're right. I am a little out of it this morning. I sense that we're close to our killer. That we've been circling round and just haven't made the connection. Let's hope this caffeine stimulates the brain."

Janet Oliver was much more on top of things than the two of us as we entered the small conference room at the station. Like almost everyone else besides Herc and me, she'd surrendered to the season by donning a bright red blouse to go with her black slacks. Her mood appeared to be as cheerful as her wardrobe. "I'm glad you came in first thing today. I have several items to report."

Herc took a chair and clapped his hands together. "Good! Our findings to date could use a boost."

Janet turned on her notebook computer. "Let's start with Muriel Fox. She's been supporting a younger sister who was paralyzed years ago in a boating accident in which her husband drowned. Their child, a boy, who was also on board, came away unscathed. At least physically. But taking in the horror of that incident seems to have affected him emotionally, which now that he's in his late teens had gotten him into trouble more than once; also signs of drug addiction. He was part of a group arrested for a break-in at a local doctor's office last year but let go for lack of evidence."

My brain attempted to put two and two together, but a clear answer wasn't coming through. "What's the tie back to Fox?"

"The doctor's office is located next to the hardware store. One of the witnesses interviewed was Terry Seiser, who told the investigating officer that, though he was at the store working that time of night, he hadn't seen anything."

Herc rested his chin on top of his folded hands. "But perhaps he had seen something. Something that could get the nephew put away for months."

"And rather than say something to the police, he spoke instead to his trusty business manager, who had been threatening to leave if he didn't clean up his act with the books," I said, following Herc's line of thinking. "Seiser could've suggested he'd suddenly remember who he saw that night if she left."

"Sounds like a pretty strong motive for murder to me," Herc said. "Thanks, Janet."

"Uh, don't get too excited yet," she replied. "Recently, the nephew entered some type of drug addiction program. As a result, he voluntarily turned himself in to the police and was let go with a warning when the doctor spoke up for him. The mother had apparently been his patient for years."

So much for that balloon. "Good catch, Janet. Seiser could've still held something like that over Fox, if it might harm the nephew's future job aspirations. Anything else?"

"Next, Carmen Loomis, the housekeeper. I couldn't find much on her at all. She's been with Seiser for almost fifteen years. Her late husband, Brian, a self-employed tinkerer, was severely injured in an industrial accident and died after lingering in the hospital for several months. No medical or life insurance. She was a good student in high school but had little training beyond a stint as a maid at a couple local motels. She met our Sergeant Buford when he was a younger officer investigating a break-in at her home, and he later gave her name to Mr. Seiser as a possible housekeeper."

"Al filled us in on most of that," Herc said.

"What's a tinkerer? Is that the same as a handyman?" I asked.

Janet returned a blank look. "I'm not sure. That's the occupation listed with the accident reports."

"That's okay. I was just curious," I replied.

"I'll see if I can find anything more on that," she said.

I would've told her not to waste her time satisfying my curiosity but knew that wouldn't stop her once there was a detail left to uncover.

"Ellen Garvey filed for divorce from Neils Garvey two months before his death but withdrew her suit a few weeks later."

"Any reason given?" I asked.

"All I could find was that the complainant had reconsidered."

"You think she learned she was soon to be a wealthy widow if she held on a little longer?" Herc asked me.

Even if that were the case, all it would mean was that Ellen Garvey wasn't quite as unimpressed by her husband's money as she'd let on. "It's possible, but that wouldn't have given her motive for killing Seiser."

"Thanks, Janet. What that does tell us is that the widow Garvey wasn't completely forthcoming with us."

"Did she also neglect to mention that until she met Seiser, she'd been romantically involved with Martin Brockhurst?" Janet asked both of us.

"No, she didn't," I replied. "Neither has indicated they've had anything but a professional relationship."

"Brockhurst certainly didn't mention it," Herc said. "We need to dig a little deeper there. Find out what happened between them and when. If the breakup came shortly after she met Seiser, we may have another motive. Brockhurst's record as a financial advisor may be clean, but that's not to say he didn't envision himself taking over that fortune for himself someday, and Seiser was an obstacle that had to be removed."

"Wow, Janet, you've given us a lot to think about and track down today," I told her, once again more than pleased with her research.

"Thanks, but I've got the easy part. I can sit here at my computer feeding it the data elements you supply and not have to deal with the personal relations part like you do."

That statement got Herc's interest. "Keep that in mind, then, when you're deciding whether to go into formal law enforcement."

"What about Cyrus Milligan?" I asked.

"I couldn't find much more about the design plan for the viewing stand. The name on it is not linked to any engineering or architectural design firm. There is no professional architect in Florida or anywhere else in this country with that name."

Herc turned to me. "That's what Val pointed out. Add that question to our to-do list for the day." Back to Janet. "Anything else?"

"Nothing related to this case, but I saw you last night, Lieutenant, when I was out admiring the Christmas lights. I didn't know you were part of a caroling group."

"Forget you ever saw me," a red-faced Herc said.

"But your group sounded so good," she replied, apparently not picking up on his discomfort.

Herc left at that point, escaping any further mention of his musical abilities. I stayed behind. "He didn't exactly volunteer to be part of that group," I told her.

She was still baffled. "But Lieutenant Morgan rarely volunteers for anything he doesn't want to do."

I gave her a knowing look. "Think about it a minute, Janet. You're exactly right."

I'd already pivoted with my hand on the doorknob when from behind me I heard her release her breath. "Oh. Right."

CHAPTER 28

"Again?" Muriel Fox said at her front door. When we didn't find her at the hardware store, we tracked her down to her home. She didn't invite us in.

"Just a few more questions based on a new piece of information," Herc said, leaning into the door well.

She blew out a huff. "All right, come in, if you must."

We wasted little time getting to the point. "Did Seiser threaten to tell the police your nephew was involved in that break-in at a doctor's office last year if you didn't stay on and help him continue to doctor the books?"

Her eyes went wide for all of a millisecond before she quickly glanced away. When she returned her gaze to us, the look of surprise had vanished. "Very good, detective. You've done some digging. As to your question, yes, Terry did exactly that. He didn't usually stick around the store much after six every evening, but that night he was there well after midnight. I'm guessing it was another night of creative bookkeeping he didn't want me to know about. Anyway, he claimed he saw Jimmy, my nephew, enter the doctor's office from a side window that was visible from across the street where Terry stood."

"When did he tell you this?" I asked.

"Months ago. Right after the break-in. Jimmy and the other two boys weren't charged officially because of lack of evidence, evidence they would've had if Terry had gone through with his threat. I stayed with the job, but I also confronted my nephew about that night, telling him there'd been a witness that could still come forward. It was enough to scare him into going straight, at least for now, and entering a program. He recently completed that program and went to the police himself."

"Did Seiser know that?" Herc asked.

"No, not that I'm aware of. With this IRS thing pending, I was about to make my move last week, tell him I was leaving and that he could no longer threaten my nephew." Realization flashed in her eyes. "Wait. You came here thinking I killed him because of that threat."

Neither of us spoke. What could we say? She was on to us.

She smiled like a kid who'd just realized her younger sibling was in more trouble than her. "I did not kill Terry Seiser."

Our next stop was Ellen Garvey, who we discovered had called an emergency meeting of the marathon committee to discuss recovery efforts. Carol McGiver, Martin Brockhurst and Cyrus Milligan were all huddled in her living room, each trying to outshout the others.

"Sorry to interrupt you folks, but we have a few more questions for some of you. Let's take advantage of you all being together. Mrs. Garvey, we'd like to first speak privately with you," Herc said, upping his volume slightly.

"Can't this wait, Lieutenant? We're in the midst of figuring out how to come back from Saturday's tragedy. We want to reschedule the marathon minus the viewing platform."

"This can't wait, Mrs. Garvey. The sooner we get some answers to our questions, the sooner we can zero in on Mr. Seiser's killer."

"That's assuming one of us is the guilty party, which isn't the case," Carol McGiver said, surveying the others as she spoke.

Herc wasn't to be deterred. "That's for us to decide, Ms.

McGiver." Back to Ellen Garvey. "The rest of you can continue your meeting, but since you're all here, don't leave until we've finished our interviews." His tone continued to make it clear that we wouldn't brook anyone choosing to do otherwise.

"My study is just down the hall," Garvey said, relenting. Once there, we took the two visitor chairs she pointed to while she chose to stand. Attempted power play. Wouldn't work. Been there, done that. "Now, what haven't we covered in the numerous times we've met since Saturday?"

"How personally involved have you been with Martin Brock-hurst?" Herc asked.

Her eyes flickered several times. "How does that part of my personal life have anything to do with Terry's murder?"

"Please answer the question, Mrs. Garvey," I said. It was the first time I'd spoken since our arrival. Herc's official status had been necessary to get this crowd moving, but now it was time for me to add my part.

She gazed at me like I'd betrayed her. "Okay, yes, Martin and I dated off and on during the last year. It was nothing serious. Mainly he acted as my escort at social occasions."

"Were you intimate?" I asked. After years of asking this question countless times, I was not the least bit apologetic.

"A few times," she replied tentatively. "I hope you don't want dates, because I didn't keep track."

"When were you last with him?" Herc asked.

She shrugged. "I can't recall. Sometime late last summer maybe."

Herc left the sensitive question to me. "Was that before or after you started seeing Terry Seiser?" I asked.

"Before. I wouldn't exactly characterize myself as a one-man woman, but it's just easier that way."

"How did Mr. Brockhurst feel about that? Did he ever express anger or resentment over losing out to him?" I asked.

She pulled a strand of hair behind her ear. "Martin has made his concerns about Terry well known ever since Terry joined our committee. He didn't think Terry added anything to our project. He has been especially vocal about the committee, me, absorbing the tab for the materials Terry initially offered to donate. But my relationship with Martin has never been that serious that he'd want to murder Terry to get rid of his rival."

I checked out Herc. He didn't appear ready to let up just yet. "Did the two men ever argue or physically exchange blows?"

"No. At least not that I'm aware."

Now Herc was done. "Thank you, Mrs. Garvey. We'll let you return to your meeting." He didn't add that I'd accompany her back to the group and pull out Brockhurst before they had a chance to exchange notes.

"I don't know what more I can tell you about Saturday," he began before he was even seated or we'd had a chance to ask our first question.

"We're more interested in your relationship with the victim before Saturday," Herc told him.

He screwed up his forehead. "Relationship? We were both on the marathon committee. That's all we had in common."

"Did you ever have words with him?" I asked.

"Did we ever argue? Sure, just like you observed when you first arrived. We all had/have different views about the best way to run the event. Several times Ellen or Carol had to break in and mediate. That's because we all wanted to pull off a successful run."

"How would you describe your personal relationship with Ellen Garvey?" I asked.

He eyed me like he couldn't believe I'd asked such a question. "Good."

"Could you expand on that?" I said. Except when we needed a specific yes or no, Herc and I weren't fans of one-word answers.

"She trusts my opinion. We like each other."

Was he purposely trying to avoid talking about dating her or just obtuse? "Have you ever been lovers?"

He shot out of his seat faster than he could pull up a spreadsheet. "That is none of your business. It has nothing to do with your investigation."

Herc had risen just as fast and blocked the doorway. Good thing he'd gone light on the doughnuts today. "Not so fast, Brockhurst. We'll decide what's pertinent to our investigation, not you."

"I want to call my attorney."

"Go ahead. You're not under arrest. We simply asked a question. Your attorney will probably advise you to cooperate even if you don't see the relevance or feel it's too personal, but we'll wait for you to make your call," Herc said firmly.

Brockhurst's shoulders slumped. "I've dated Ellen on occasion. More like when she needed an escort to some social event. I'm a professional. I know it's not the smartest move for a financial advisor to get involved too personally with their client because they could easily lose their impartiality."

"How did you feel about her personal relationship with Terry Seiser?" Herc asked.

"Did I like it? No. Was I happy for her? Not in the least. I've already told you what I thought about the guy. He was so out of her league."

I asked the obvious. "Were you jealous?"

"No. I have more self-respect than that. I asked Ellen more than once what she saw in the guy, and she never gave me a very good response. I tolerated the two of them together because I was sure it wouldn't last. He was bound to screw up at some point and then she'd see the light."

We released Brockhurst and spent a few minutes comparing Garvey's responses with his before calling for the next interviewee.

"What are your vibes telling you about those two?" Herc asked after he'd closed the door.

"We caught them both off guard about their relationship. Each reacted about like we could've predicted: stalling until reminded we had every right to ask, insulted that we asked, and then when neither of those reactions worked, attempted cooperation. I'd say

Garvey's response was closer to her actual feelings than Brock-hurst's, who's hiding the depth of his feelings for the woman. But did I pick up on anything, especially from him, that suggested he killed Seiser out of jealousy? No. We don't have anything on which to arrest him."

Herc collapsed in his chair and pawed his cheeks. "That's about where I am."

"Process of elimination, Herc. That's something."

"Yeah, think positive. Except I'm not quite ready to take Garvey off the list since she wound up as the only beneficiary."

"Beneficiary of what, though?" I pointed out. "A failing business and modest residence. Unless there's some unknown treasure hidden in one of them, she doesn't need them."

"Okay, let's move on to Milligan." He checked his phone. "Looks like Oliver has done it again."

What had our trusty researcher found now? I stole a glance at my own phone and smiled after reading her text. Our interview of Milligan had just taken on additional significance.

Milligan couldn't sit still once seated, and he kept gnawing on a fingernail. Rather than protest this additional interview as the prior two had, he waited for us to begin.

"We've been researching other marathons around the country and haven't been able to find anything like the design plan you submitted to the committee. Where did you find it?"

"The name's on it. Did you check him out?" he replied.

"We tried," I said. "Couldn't find anyone by that name in any engineering or architectural firm in this country or on the registers of any of those organizations."

He opened his palms. "Sorry. That's all I can tell you."

"Try again," Herc said.

"The signature's hard to read. Maybe you got the spelling wrong?"

"It's time to come clean, Milligan. Here's what we think happened. By some twist of fate, you were contacted by Martin Brockhurst on the recommendation of his brother, Wally, who briefly served as the group's consultant without success. Wally knew you not as a marathon consultant but as a fellow runner to whom he owed gambling money. The committee failed to do its due diligence on you, and somehow you got hired."

"Where'd you get all this information?" Milligan asked, neither confirming nor denying Herc's speculation.

"We've got a crackerjack research team back at the station. You were able to bluff your way through the initial committee meetings, but eventually you ran out of tricks to impress them. And then out of the blue, you suggested the viewing stand even though you'd never seen one at a marathon. Like you told us, you'd observed something like it at a political rally, but you weren't able to find anything online. Then you got creative and found some student to put together the plan, thinking you'd find some way to back away from the idea later."

Milligan had stopped the beaver act on his fingernail but was now rubbing his thighs back and forth.

Herc surprised me with how well he'd absorbed Val's thought regarding the viewing stand.

"To your horror, Terry Seiser stepped forward and volunteered to build the platform. The guy owned a hardware store and a lumberyard and was offering to provide the materials free of cost. Why not assume he knew what he was doing, even though he was working with an untested plan from an amateur?"

"The committee assumed that, not just me," he returned, as if that excused his irresponsible action.

"This student or whoever put the plan together, do they have any architectural or engineering background?" I asked even though Milligan hadn't really admitted to any of Herc's hypothesis. He seemed to believe we knew more than we did, one of Herc's talents.

"Don't blame him for that thing falling. Seiser didn't know what he was doing."

"I wasn't getting at that," I replied. "The plan looked real enough." It had fooled both Val and me. "I just wanted to know if the creator knew anything about design."

He hesitated slightly, apparently debating how much he should reveal. "He's a second-year student in the architectural engineering program at the local community college. I, uh, got his name off the internet."

I'd gone through that same program a few years back once I recuperated from my on-the-job accident. I'd been impressed with the training I received even though I moved on to interior design. I didn't know if I was relieved to hear the designer at least had that much cred or impressed that they got away with it.

"That's it? You didn't vet his credentials?" I asked, marveling more and more how little oversight the committee had over this guy.

"Well, yeah. We talked online. More than once, especially when Seiser threw that wrench in the works by saying the structure had to be portable for future use." He paused. "Actually, that came from his assistant, now that I think about it."

"Assistant?" Herc and I both asked in unison.

"Yeah, some woman. Said she was working with him on the project."

"Can you describe her?" I asked.

"I only talked to her on the phone. Older, creaky-like voice. Sounded like she knew what she was talking about."

"When was this?" Herc asked.

He stopped rubbing his thighs and massaged the back of his neck instead. "Recently. Two weeks ago maybe?"

"And she's the one who insisted it be easy to disassemble?" Herc said.

"Yeah, now that you mention it. Her, not Seiser. Are we done here? I need to get back to that meeting and find out if I still have a job."

"You can go, but we may have more questions."

"Yeah, sure," Milligan said as he backed out the door.

The two of us sat staring at each other for several seconds before either of us spoke.

"Three days of talking to this large cast of characters and the subject of Seiser having a female assistant never came up," I said, still in shock.

"Until now. That's why they taught us long ago that it wasn't over until that gem of a clue emerged out of nowhere."

"Are you thinking what I'm thinking?" I asked.

"Not yet. The other thing they taught us was not to assume until all the evidence was in."

He picked up his phone and texted Janet, requesting she get together Milligan's phone records for the last month. He also asked for the same thing for all the women we'd interviewed in this case. And he put a rush on the entire package.

CHAPTER 29

y the time we arrived at the station, Janet Oliver had the requested information ready for our review. With her help, we crosschecked Milligan's incoming phone calls against the numbers of the women we'd already interviewed. We expected to find Ellen Garvey's number on the list, and it was. We did not find any instances of Carol McGiver calling him.

Nor did we find Muriel Fox's number, either her own personal number or the number of the hardware store's phone. We'd pretty much eliminated her as a suspect but needed to verify our conclusion.

Although the unknown woman could've used a burner phone to contact the man, we didn't need to check out that theory, because we found two calls from Carmen Loomis.

I stared at the data long past reading her name. It made sense, and yet I couldn't quite get my head around the idea. "Carmen Loomis, the housekeeper, the loyal, longtime employee is our killer," I said, saying it out loud to make it seem more real.

"Alleged killer," Herc said. "All we have is Milligan's statement and the fact that she apparently called him twice during the period he gave us. A good attorney would argue she could've called him for any number of reasons instead of what he claimed. Or someone else could've used her phone."

"Sounds like another visit is in order. We have to learn her side of the story."

We thanked Janet for pulling the data together so quickly and took off to once again to question the housekeeper.

An unknown car was parked in front of the house. Herc called in the plates. The car belonged to Ellen Garvey. "Do you suppose she feels guilty about inheriting the house?" he asked.

"Perhaps, but I'm getting weird vibes about her being here. My palms itch."

No one came to the door when we rang. The blinds had been drawn in the front room to prevent anyone from seeing in.

"Looks like she doesn't want company," I whispered.

"Say something out loud to indicate we're giving up and leaving."

"Why don't you?" I whispered back.

"You're a better actress."

"She doesn't appear to be in, Herc," I said in my theater voice.

"Let's go," he replied.

We drove around the block and parked in the alley a few houses down from Seiser's. We made our way cautiously to the back of the house to what must be the housekeeper's private entrance. The door was locked, but with a little creative jimmying on Herc's part, he got it open.

He turned back to me, now whispering also. "Stay behind me, since only I have a gun."

I was only too happy to follow suit. Even if I wasn't allowed to carry for legal reasons as a consultant to the department, I'd chosen not to be armed.

Just as a precaution, Herc called for backup before entering. But we didn't wait for them to show up. If Ellen Garvey was in there, we didn't know in what state we'd find Loomis.

We moved swiftly through her private quarters until we heard her voice in the kitchen.

"Sign it. Then you can be on your merry way," Loomis said in a demanding, authoritative voice we hadn't heard from her before.

"It won't be legal. You know that, Mrs. Loomis," Ellen Garvey said. "I was ready to give you the house when I came here. That won't happen if you kill me."

"Like you would've ever turned the place over to me. You want it all to yourself. Just like you wanted Terry. After all the years I gave that man, hoping he'd fall in love with me someday, you couldn't let that happen."

"You've been fooling yourself. He only kept you on because you worked so cheap."

"Yeah, I heard him that day when you asked him about me. He said I was an ugly troll. Thanks to you, that was the day I decided he didn't deserve me anymore. In fact, he didn't deserve to live. The responsibility for his death rests with you."

"Me? I didn't sabotage the viewing stand. I don't know how you did it, but apparently you figured out how to make it collapse."

"It was easy, once I got my own copy of the plan. Even convinced that yoyo in charge of the race to have it drawn up so it would come down with just a few turns of the screw, or in this case, bolts. I learned a few things from my late husband, who was a handyman. Terry never questioned how minor repairs got made around this place. He certainly didn't know how. All I had to do was get there that morning before he did and loosen things. Once I got him under the platform, I just had to undo one more bolt and pull away the flooring with a rope I attached to my car."

"You won't get away with this," Garvey said. Surprisingly, her voice still carried authority. Perhaps her days as a teacher were now helping her keep her cool.

We'd heard enough. Time to rescue the hostage.

Herc motioned for me to remain behind.

He threw the door wide and raced inside. "Hold it right …"

I heard a heavy crash and the thud of his gun flying loose.

"We've been waiting for you, Lieutenant. Even greased the floor as a sort of welcome gift," Carmen Loomis said in that same new tone, commanding, unafraid and snide. Gone was the mouse we'd dealt with before.

"You won't get away with this, Mrs. Loomis," Herc said in a slightly breathless tone. "There's more police waiting outside."

A bluff, but he had to try something to even the odds now that he'd lost his gun.

Apparently it didn't work. "You might as well join us, Mrs. Summerfield. I've got my gun on your partner," she called.

I thought fast, trying to figure a way out of this one. Nothing was coming to me other than to make her think she had the upper hand. No problem there, since she did.

I took a stab at bravado. "I don't relish falling on my keister like my partner did. I'll just make myself at home in here. This is your space, if I recall. You'll have to flee once you've done your damage in there, but I can't believe you'd go without taking some of your personal things with you. Maybe something of your late husband's you've retained all these years?"

I was pulling the dragon's teeth, but that was the plan. Draw her attention away from Herc and Garvey. I hunkered down behind an easy chair and the wall opposite the door, anticipating her reaction. She didn't let me down. Three shots flew through the open doorway. As a recruit many years ago, I'd learned how to take cover when approaching a suspect with a gun. That training had come back to me now.

As I'd hoped, that was all the time Herc needed. I heard a loud thump and the sound of a body crashing to the ground. *Please let it be Loomis.*

"It's okay, Ro. She's out cold. I found a skillet on the kitchen counter and took her down."

I took my time getting up from behind the chair and heading to the kitchen, treading carefully around the area where she'd spilled grease. Ellen Garvey slumped against the back of a chair. Her legs had been tied together with a rope.

"You okay, Ro?" Herc asked. "I knew what you were doing and just hoped you'd gotten away from the door."

"It'll take a while for my heart to slow, but yes, I'm fine otherwise. How about you? Did you break anything when you went flying?"

"Maybe a bruise or two on my behind, but the main damage was to my ego. I shoulda anticipated a trap like that. She's wilier than I realized."

I turned my attention to Ellen Garvey, untying her legs. "How about you, Ellen? Did she hurt you?"

"I'll be fine once my legs come back to life. Thank you both. So much. I thought I was a goner."

"Why are you here?" I asked.

"She called and asked me to come discuss disposal of the house. She was interested in buying it. I'd been considering turning it over to her for a dollar. I didn't need it. I don't know what Terry had been thinking, changing his will. I didn't feel guilty being the recipient, but I wanted to make things right. Then she pulled a gun on me."

"From what we heard, it sounded like she'd drawn up a document transferring ownership to her," Herc said.

"I tried to tell her it wouldn't be legal, but for all I know she copied something off the internet that would've held up. I have no idea how she planned to get rid of me if I signed it, other than she obviously had no compunction about killing me."

The backup team arrived, and Herc turned Loomis over to them, once she regained consciousness and he'd read her her rights.

We stayed with Ellen Garvey a little longer to assure she had fully recovered from her ordeal.

"I still can't believe she was the one who made that platform collapse," she said as she rubbed her ankles where the rope had been.

I was about to agree with her but decided not to let on Herc and I were still working through that one ourselves.

A search of Loomis's car turned up not only a copy of the design plan for the platform but also a tool box that included a wrench, the probable weapon used to knock Seiser unconscious. Though it had been wiped clean, further analysis in the lab would most likely reveal traces of blood, human hair and other organic matter.

"I knew he wasn't a good person," Carmen Loomis said when we questioned her at the station after she'd found an attorney. "But I believed the love of a good woman could change him. That's why I stayed with him all those years. Not so much loyalty as the hope that we'd eventually be together, even when he'd take up with other women. Those relationships never lasted." She offered a self-satisfied smile. "He always came home to me."

"What was different about Ellen Garvey?" I asked.

"She had money. I sensed but didn't know for sure the business was suffering. That guy who runs the lumberyard for him came to the house a couple times. Terry made me go to my quarters, but I listened in. The lumberyard guy accused him of stealing from the profits. Terry denied it, of course, but the guy wouldn't let it go, even when Terry threatened to fire him."

Gordo Zaharian hadn't mentioned those visits, but then, we'd only interviewed him once and hadn't pressed.

Herc asked the question of the day. "If you loved him so much, why did you kill him?"

She took her time answering, like she'd been rehearsing this speech. "A woman can only take so much abuse. Not that he ever hurt me physically, but when I heard him dismissing my worth to that woman, I finally realized I'd been a fool to put up with him all these years. He wasn't going to change."

I'd followed her reasoning up to that point. But the leap from disillusionment to murder didn't make sense. "Why didn't you just quit? Your domestic skills could've gotten you a job at much higher pay with numerous employers."

"I was afraid to try. Over the years, Terry had repeatedly told me I had no skills. He was only keeping me on out of pity. I'd come to believe him. Plus, I loved the house. I saw it as mine more than his. I was the one who took care of it."

"When did you decide to kill him?" I asked.

"I told you. When he put me down to Ellen Garvey. She took it upon herself to tell him I was in love with him. He laughed. Laughed at the idea of ever being with me! But that wasn't enough. He called me an old, used-up hag that no man would ever want to touch."

She'd been so cool and distant when responding to our questions thus far. But now tears filled her eyes and ran down her face. "I guess I snapped when I heard him describe me that way. He had to go. He had to pay for what he'd said."

"But why go to such lengths knocking down the viewing stand when there were so many other ways you could've killed him?" Herc asked.

She sighed. "I must have thought of them all that first day after hearing him insult me to her. Poison, stabbing, gas. My husband gave me that gun for protection whenever he was out on a late-night call. I stashed it away years ago and only got it out to threaten Ellen Garvey. I wanted to humiliate Terry as much as he'd humiliated me. He'd been so engrossed constructing that platform, I decided that would be my revenge."

"You murdered him for revenge?" I said, attempting to put a bow on her motive.

"Yes, but I also wanted the house. I deserved it after all my years of faithful service for such a pittance."

"Then you learned he'd changed his will," Herc said.

She scoffed. "His final insult. I doubt he suspected I wanted to kill him. Changing his will was just one more way he could exert his power over those who'd been there for him all these years."

There wasn't much more to say after that. We'd let the county attorney put together the rest of the case from the array of evidence we'd collected. She'd given us her confession, and there was also Ellen Garvey's testimony about being held hostage and forced to give away the house.

"Ya wanna unwind before calling it a day?" Herc asked.

"I don't feel like celebrating. I need to process what we've just gone through."

"I get it. Let's just hang out in the small conference room and debrief. What's on your mind?"

I took my time working through my thoughts until I could finally put them into words. "How many homicides have we worked over the years? Too many to count. I've never come across what I'd characterize as a 'good murder.' Even in this case, with a man who was liked by few, it still wasn't necessary. He took advantage of a woman who asked no more from him than his appreciation of what she did to make his life more comfortable. Finally, she'd had enough."

He didn't respond at once. He appeared to be thinking through my comments. "I'm not saying she asked for it," he said at last, "but like you pointed out to her, she could've left at any time."

"But that's the saddest part of this case. He played on her lack of self-confidence and convinced her she couldn't survive without his benevolence."

"And now she'll never find out because she'll be the guest of the state, probably for the rest of her life," Herc said.

We sat in silence several minutes. I needed to find something positive about this case before I could put a period on it, but I was struggling to think of anything.

"After all these years together, I think I can read your mind, Ro. It's almost Christmas, and this year you've allowed yourself to get into the spirit of the season. This case, even now that we've found our killer, runs counter to all those good thoughts. Try this on for size: the marathon may not have come off as planned, but they still raised a lot of money for the cause and will raise even more with a rescheduled marathon."

"True. For low-income housing. Doesn't the irony strike you?" I replied, still unable to shake my mood.

"Enlighten me."

"The motive in this case revolved around a woman who had very little going for her in her life except the home she took care of. She was the embodiment of the client Ellen Garvey and Carol McGiver believe they are serving."

"I can't let you leave here until we've found some light at the end of this tunnel."

"Help me find it, then, Herc. I really do want to put this case behind me and enjoy the spirit of the season."

"What have you always told me when I was in the dumps?" he asked.

Elbows on the table, I cradled my face in my palms. "My sage advice escapes me at the moment."

"Take the situation and turn it upside down," he said.

"We already discussed that contingency. She should've left him years ago."

He stared me down. "Try again."

"C'mon, Herc."

"You wanna get home to Deli Man to enjoy the next several days of the holiday?"

Of course I did. He was right. I just had to refocus. "What good things came out of this investigation? First and foremost, expensive viewing stands aren't needed for marathons. If such a thing even exists."

"Good start. Keep going."

"Although I hate to give him credit, like Daryl Henson advised, any future attempt to stage a marathon should focus more on security."

"Now you're cookin'."

"Any future attempts to stage a marathon should also include a consultant who knows what he or she is doing." Cyrus Milligan should be run out of town.

Three attempts but no home runs. I returned to the ironic statement I'd made earlier. Then it came to me.

"Turn the situation upside down," I said. "Ellen Garvey and Carol McGiver should point out to potential donors what could happen if individuals, women like Carmen Loomis, feel they have no future. Then and only then does the need for low-income housing become real."

"There you go! You've done it again."

"Thanks, Herc. Merry Christmas."

EPILOGUE

lthough I was feeling much better about the resolution of the Seiser case by the time I got home, Chuck seemed to sense discovering the killer had taken a toll on me. He didn't push to go out and take in more holiday events like he had of late. Instead, he brought home comfort food from the restaurant and had a bottle of white wine chilling.

I deferred on the wine for a while but dove into the meat loaf and mac and cheese. "I don't know how you did it, but you knew exactly how to get me past the last several hours," I said as I finished my second helping of the mac and cheese.

"I have to give Morgan some credit. He texted me just before I was headed home and alerted me to your mood. What he referred to as 'post-climax letdown.'" He raised a brow. "What exactly do you guys do to celebrate catching your culprit?"

It took me a second to understand his comment. I had to snort when it penetrated my exhausted brain that Herc had unintentionally made it sound like there'd been some hanky-panky involved in wrapping the case. "He meant well. The case took a lot out of us."

"Given his text, I conferred with my staff on meal recommendations."

"Give them my thanks tomorrow," I told him, truly appreciative.

He gazed at me thoughtfully as I sipped my coffee. "This part of your investigative activities is new to me. You've never been down when past cases ended. In fact, you've always been ready to celebrate. What's different this time? Is it the impending holiday?"

I gave him the headline version of what I'd told Herc earlier. "One of the abilities I've developed over the years as I've interviewed suspects has been to ask myself who saw their situations so untenable they saw ending their adversary's life as their only solution. Fortunately, not many scenarios are that dire."

"Where are you going with that?" Chuck asked, taking me seriously.

"I understand why Carmen Loomis felt she had no other choice but to end Seiser's life, but it didn't have to be that way. He was never going to change. She knew that, although she said at first that she stayed with him hoping she could do just that. But finally, she admitted she didn't see that she had any other alternative. That's what concerns me. She shouldn't have reached that point. Not that I'm faulting her. Not entirely. She fell through the system. That's the part that bothers me."

"You're not blaming yourself for that, are you?"

"Only as much as I'm part of that system."

He lifted the coffee carafe. "More?" He refilled his mug. "Where does that leave you tonight? You want to continue discussing Carmen Loomis?"

I considered his question. I wasn't ready to move on from the Seiser case just yet, but tonight I needed to distance myself. For a little bit, anyhow. "Actually, I'd like to sit back and cuddle with you this evening. Maybe watch a Christmas flick?"

"I can't think of anything I'd like better," he replied, taking my hand in his.

I'd seen the movie at least three times before, but that was just what I needed, something familiar and comfortable. Chuck fit that description also. As well as Jason, who'd finessed a spot between the two of us on the sofa. This was exactly where I wanted to be tonight.

And later, snuggled up in bed with Chuck. I wanted to be there too.

I slept well and even allowed myself an extra half hour of sleep in the morning.

Chuck peeked in from the bathroom, fresh from the shower. "Good morning. How do you feel today?"

That wasn't just morning chitchat. Today his question held particular significance.

"As a matter of fact, Chuck, yes, I feel ready to move on."

Once I'd had breakfast and spent some long overdue quality time with Jason, I called Ellen Garvey and made an appointment to see her in an hour.

"I'm so glad you're here," she said when we were back in the same living room Herc and I visited the day before. "I want to thank you and your partner again for saving my life yesterday. I thought that woman was about to kill me."

"It all came together just in time," I replied.

"How did you figure it out?"

"We went back over the design plan for the viewing stand with Cyrus Milligan, and during that review he mentioned the woman who'd contacted him a few weeks ago requesting a copy. She referred to herself as Seiser's assistant."

"He didn't have an assistant," she cut in.

"Exactly. After a little tracking of phone records, Carmen Loomis came to the top of the list."

"That was some quick thinking on your part when she had me and your partner trapped in the kitchen. Letting her think you might destroy her personal items."

"Thanks. I knew we'd all be toast if I ran into the kitchen."

"How did you know to duck the bullets she sent your way?" Garvey asked.

"Training. But Lieutenant Morgan was responsible for the takedown. I was banking on my being able to distract her long enough for him to get the gun away from her."

"You work well together."

"It comes with time."

"I owe you. If there's ever anything I can do to help your future investigations, just let me know."

The entrée I'd been hoping for. "Actually, there is something you can do. Not for me. As part of your low-income housing program."

"Oh?" Did she sound curious or suspicious?

"I've been thinking a lot about Carmen Loomis since we arrested her. I acknowledge up front, she's guilty of first-degree murder. She planned it and carried it out. She's also guilty of kidnapping you and holding two law enforcement officers at gunpoint. Even given all that, I haven't been able to stop thinking that it didn't have to be." I shared the same thoughts with her that I'd laid out with Herc and later with Chuck.

I wasn't sure what kind of reception I'd receive when I finished. If it didn't fly, so be it. There might be other ways to pursue my concern.

"If I understand you, you're suggesting Project Phoenix go beyond just providing low-cost income housing for individuals in need. You think we should be addressing the root causes of their need."

"Your summary is right on point, Ellen."

She was silent for several beats. Thinking of how she could let me down gently?

"The Loomis woman didn't get me to her house at gunpoint. I went willingly, because I'd planned to sign the house over to her. If she'd just waited long enough for me to tell her as much. But she was desperate. Plus, I was the woman who'd taken Terry away from her. Or so she saw it. But all that aside, you're right. She would have been the type of candidate for our program."

"I'm not here to tell you how to run the program, but I appreciate your hearing me out."

I made ready to leave.

"Wait, I can't afford to let the passion you expressed walk out the door without asking you to join our group."

"I, uh, thanks, but it's time for me to get back to my real job of interior design. My daughter has been doing double duty keeping our company afloat."

She cocked her head. "You're an interior designer?"

I told her about Nailed It Home Renos, hoping she'd understand why I couldn't sign on.

She understood all right, just from a different perspective. "You convert old, rundown houses into beautiful new homes?"

"Yes, that's right."

"Mrs. Summerfield, Rowena, you more than anyone else understands the healing and spiritual awakening power of a new home. I'm thinking about this as I go, but we need your expertise. You wouldn't have to participate full time. Perhaps sit on our board, or if that's too formal, consult for us. Inspire potential donors the same way you just spoke to me."

"I—I don't know what to say. I've been juggling part-time homicide investigations with my rehab business the way it is. I don't know how I could possibly work in another commitment."

She rose and came to me, taking my hand. "You need to catch your breath after solving this big murder case. And we're heading right into the holidays. Take a few days to think through my offer. I'll call you once things have settled down."

"Uh, okay." That's about all I could get out. I almost ran from that living room.

I spent the rest of the day helping Val put the finishing touches on Mehaffy House. There was little left for me to do, since I'd determined the layout, paint colors, wallpaper selections, appliances and hardware some time ago. My main task now was to stage it. Most of the furniture was pieces I'd acquired over time at estate sales and stored in the warehouse quarters within our office building.

"I'm so glad you finished your case in time to help me finish up here," Val said.

"Me, too," I replied as I shoved a loveseat a few inches to the left. "I had no qualms about your being able to execute my staging plans, but I really wanted to be here myself."

She stood back to take in our surroundings. "I have to admit, I wasn't sure how this combination of modern with traditional would play out in this old house, but as usual, you were right on top of things."

"I took a chance with the pale lavender and rose walls. I didn't want the first floor to come off as too feminine."

"Amanda is anxious to put the place on the market. Even though the first of the year isn't the best time to sell, she claims she already has a couple buyers lined up," Val said.

"We do need to sell to recoup our investment, but I've grown rather attached to the place even though I haven't been able to spend as much time here as I would've liked."

Val wandered around the downstairs, her hand trailing over one piece of furniture after another. At one point, she pulled up and pivoted to face me. "Why don't we throw a party before we turn it over? It's a little late, but we could put something together for New Year's Eve if we limited the guest list to our small circle of friends."

"That's a great idea. Do you think we could get Amanda on board?"

She laughed. "If Jim invites some of his bachelor officers, yes."

Then I remembered my new commitment to helping those less fortunate in the community. How did a fancy New Year's Eve bash relate? "Let's just keep this simple, okay?"

She took a step back, eyes narrowed. "Okay, fine. What aren't you telling me?"

I wasn't ready to share my recent epiphany yet. It was too new and still evolving. But I needed to say something. Val had particularly good mother-reading radar. "Let's just say I'm still coming down from this last case. The whole point of the marathon was to raise money to support Project Phoenix, which helps lower-income people afford their own homes. I was so focused on discovering the killer, it only struck me yesterday that you and I made a similar commitment to helping lower income residents in the community improve their own properties."

"That was just weeks ago, Mom. You got busy with the Reindeer Run Rendezvous and then the Seiser murder, and I've been involved wrapping up this house, although we did spiff up the entrances to the two neighboring properties."

"Let's count those as a win and enter the new year keeping our eyes open to other possibilities." I let it go at that, other than suggesting she plan the party and I'd go in halfsies.

"Speaking of new possibilities," she said, "how about a project closer to home? Would you be terribly upset if Jim and I sold my half of the duplex? We want a bigger place, and I'd prefer not to live in his current house, which he shared with his late wife. He'll put it on the market too."

I attempted to take in her announcement. Our cozy side-by-side arrangement was coming to an end. I thought I'd be the one to eventually move out of the duplex, because Chuck wanted our "own" place. "Why don't you buy Mehaffy House?" I said kiddingly, although I rather liked the idea.

"No, although we've discussed moving in here a few times. But we both want a more modern house and just one story. We've got our eyes on one not too far from Luke Jarvis's mini-mansion. It could be Nailed It's next project."

Wow. Just wow. The world had begun to spin faster. "Does this mean …?"

"That we're talking marriage? Maybe someday. We'll split the cost of the house and rehabbing it all legal-like, but neither of us is ready to make it formal yet. I'll still pop by to look after Jason whenever you want, if you're worried about that?"

"Honestly, I hadn't gotten that far yet. I'm still envisioning what it will be like without you so close by."

"It's been a good arrangement since Dad passed, and your accident and my divorce. We needed each other. But now we're each in a better place emotionally."

"I'm pleased for you. And Jim. Really. Just give me a day or so to get used to the idea. As for our next project, I can't think of any house I'd rather make into a home."

Chuck was already at the duplex when I got there late afternoon. He was working shorter hours now that the case was over.

"I suspected something like that was coming," he said after I'd updated him about Val and Jim's plans. "Jim intimated something like that when we played golf last week. How do you feel about this change?"

"Let's just say I'm getting used to the idea."

"Funny, at one time I thought you and I would be the ones moving out."

"Have you given up on that idea?" I asked, not sure I wanted to hear his response.

"Honestly, no. I'm still hopeful the idea will appeal to you at some point too. But in the meantime, this is my new home, although I'm still waiting for the right time to ask that question I brought up the other night."

He was circling the wagons, asking without asking if it was okay to broach it now. I knew I couldn't avoid it much longer, but I needed just a little more time to clarify my feelings. "I love how patient you're being with me, Chuck. I love you. That's for sure. It's just that there's been so much happening the last two days, I want your question to get the response it deserves. Can you give me a day? There's something I must do first."

"A day makes it Christmas Eve. Can you handle my question amidst all the other celebrating?"

"Yes. I believe I can."

CHRISTMAS EVE DAY DAWNED BRIGHT AND CRISP, A PERFECT December day in Florida. I left the duplex early, before Jason was even up and on patrol.

Other than a groundskeeper, no one else was at the cemetery this early in the morning. I parked and made my way quickly to the columbarium that held Ben's remains. I no longer came here often as I adjusted to life without my late husband. I'd come to realize I didn't have to be here to communicate with him.

But today was a different story. I needed the physical reminder of his passing to think through my situation.

"You gave me your blessing to move on once you left this earth," I said, my hand touching the compartment that held his remains. "At the time, I never thought this day would come. What we had was so special, I couldn't picture anyone else taking your place. Chuck doesn't want to do that, and I don't expect him to. But I've come to love him, Ben. He has become a critical part of my life."

I didn't feel the least bit uncomfortable talking to a wall. I had to say what I'd come to say. "I know you're always with me in spirit, and I would never do anything to ruin the beautiful relationship we had. But after all this time, I'm ready to head into a new future.

"I don't need your blessing. You gave me that long ago. I'm here because I need closure. You'll always be in my heart. But I now know there's room there for Chuck too."

I touched the compartment one last time, and as I turned to leave, my heart lightened.

I was ready to move on.

LATER IN THE DAY, I RECEIVED A TEXT FROM ELLEN GARVEY.

Just wanted you to know I'm following through on our discussion about the properties and businesses I inherited from Terry. I've talked to my attorney about turning over the hardware store to Muriel Fox and the lumberyard to Gordo Zaharian. My attorney suggested they each pay a dollar, so both transactions will be seen as legitimate purchases. The IRS has already contacted me about bookkeeping questions Terry had been avoiding for months, which will hold up the transfer of the business to Fox until that issue has been satisfactorily addressed. My attorney has agreed to help her deal with them. I'd like to make Terry's house a Project Phoenix home. Hopefully, you and your partner will consider rehabbing it.

I hope you're seriously considering my offer to serve on my board. I truly believe your presence will be good for both of us and for the clients we serve.

The Reindeer Run is on again! The committee, minus Cyrus Milligan and, of course, Terry, has agreed to stay together and hold the marathon in late January.

Talk more after the holidays.

Not only was she doing something about the unfairness of Seiser's bequest, she wasn't wasting any time getting to it. Whether she was doing that for my benefit to convince me to sign on with her or she was just that efficient, her actions were impressive.

I'd keep them in mind as I considered joining her board.

"Who wants more ham?" Chuck asked the group gathered around my dining room table on Christmas Day.

Herc was the first to hold out his plate. "Since you're offering. This is delicious, Dawson."

"Thank the kitchen staff at The Sandpiper. I gave them last night and today off, even though a lot of folks like to celebrate the holiday at a restaurant," Chuck replied. "My people have worked hard this holiday season and will put in a full night and day next week on New Year's, so today and last night are for them."

"And those of us who benefited from the time off thank you, Chuck," Shane Bolton said.

"We're glad you could join us today," I told him, my relief that he hadn't been the killer underlying my comment.

Today's meal was a far cry from our Thanksgiving meal. Val and Jim had done their darnedest to get me past my mad at Herc and Jim that day, and I'd finally succumbed, but today it was Chuck's and my turn to host the meal.

I was so happy I could hardly breathe as I gazed around the table at our guests. Val and Jim, of course. Herc and Luann, both wearing mysterious grins. Shane. Lorna. Amanda.

Ryder had taken his newfound sister, Melinda, on a Caribbean cruise. I still had trouble picturing Ryder sunning himself around a pool on deck, but he wanted to treat his sister to something she'd never done before.

"Who wants to share what they got for Christmas?" Chuck asked, enjoying his role of host. Only I knew he couldn't wait to tell them about my gift.

"Luann and I were on the same wavelength," Herc said, taking the lead. "She gave me tickets to the Ossie Boseman concert next month."

"Who's Ossie Boseman?" Amanda asked, trying to appear interested but clearly out of her element.

"You don't know who Ossie Boseman is?" Herc replied incredulously. "Only the coolest jazz saxophonist this century. I don't know where she got the idea how much I liked his stuff."

"Like you haven't listened to his CD every time we were in your car," Luann said, chuckling like a proud parent.

"How about you, Luann?" Val asked. "How did our boy do?"

"Your *boy* got me a destination gift, tickets to see the antique extravaganza in Mount Dora next month. And he's willing to attend with me, even though he's not much for old furniture."

"Points for you, man," Jim said, slapping Herc on the back.

There was no mention of an overnight stay—something the two of them wanted to keep to themselves, which went a long way toward telling me how far things had progressed between them.

"Jim and I are planning to sell my half of the duplex and his old house and buy another one, which we'll renovate," Val announced.

"That's why we went light on gifts this year," Jim added, "although we're planning a trip to New York City this spring to see a few shows."

"Congratulations!" Luann said. "We're happy for you, aren't we, Herc?"

"Uh, yeah. That's great news," he said, the idea of seeing a Broadway show almost as far from his to-do list as a trip to the moon.

"Have you decided what shows to see yet?" Amanda asked.

"No, the trip is a last-minute add-on, when our tree looked so bare," Jim said. "I'll let Valerie make that decision."

Shane took his turn next. "My parents were appalled by the sparseness of my apartment when they visited a while back, so they've given me a gift certificate for a bed and mattress. All they wanted in return was for me to promise I'd visit them this spring."

Amanda didn't let that comment go by. "Do you need help shopping for them?"

"Thanks, but I thought I'd order online."

"Are you sure that's the best way to determine what kind of mattress you need?" She wasn't one to give up easily. I had to stifle a laugh as I pictured just how Amanda would go about helping him check out mattresses.

"I'll call you if it comes to that." The shopping junket probably wouldn't materialize, but I had to give her credit for trying.

Apparently Shane's parents weren't the only ones to be concerned about their offspring's lifestyle. "My parents gave me a year's subscription to one of those TV streaming services," Amanda said. "I guess they think I spend too many nights out partying. They hope I'll stay home to watch movies. I'm still a young woman with plenty of life in me, and I should be out enjoying myself." Her comment was aimed at Shane, who was studying his mashed sweet potatoes.

I caught Val rolling her eyes. Like her, Amanda was in her mid-thirties. Nightly rounds of the bars were no longer part of her routine. Those ended before Jim came along.

"I treated myself to a gift this year," Lorna said. Her brother had been a murder victim months ago. Although Herc and I had identified the killer, it was taking her time to adjust to his loss. I was glad she'd decided to join us today. I'd been afraid she'd just hole up in her condo, feeling sorry for herself.

"What was that?" Val asked.

Lorna held up her right hand. "This gold bracelet. I wanted something personal, and it was a way to support my brother's old college friend Coral Neely. She's a jewelry designer who's recently switched to gold."

"Good for you," Herc told her. "Ro and I saw some of her work when we were working your brother's case."

"Rowena got me some art also," Chuck said, the delight he'd shown when he'd unwrapped my package still apparent in his tone. "Watercolors of the exteriors of each of my three businesses. What did you call them, Ro?"

"A triptych," I replied. Weeks ago, I'd gone through Luke Jarvis, another suspect in the murder of Lorna's brother and a performance artist, to find a local artist who'd be willing to paint them by Christmas. I didn't know how she'd managed to visit each of the establishments more than once to sketch them without Chuck finding out, but he swore he'd never seen her.

Chuck bolted over to the Christmas tree where he'd left them and brought back the paintings to show our guests.

"These are great, boss," Shane said. "I can see every little detail of the front of The Sandpiper."

"The same for The Piper," Lorna said. "Will you hang each one in its respective eatery?"

"I'm still deciding," Chuck said. "Maybe in my office at the restaurant instead, since they're intended to be shown together."

"You haven't told us what Chuck got you," Herc said once admiration of Chuck's new artwork died down.

Chuck glanced at me expectantly. "I was doubly blessed," I replied. Now it was my turn to retrieve my gifts from under the tree.

"Ooh, I recognize the logo on that box," Val said excitedly.

Chuck had cleared a space on the table, where I set the box. I lifted out a filmy piece of rose chiffon, a cocktail dress that had been designed and made just for me by our recent client Bergitta Tornwald.

Val squealed. "Mom! It's gorgeous."

"It is, isn't it?"

"Not that your mom's wardrobe needed that much improvement, but if she's gonna join the upper crust of the community by being on the board of Project Phoenix, she'll need some fancy duds for all their events."

"You're joining Ellen Garvey's board?" Herc said, nearly knocking over his water glass.

"Chuck is a little ahead of himself. I haven't said yes yet, but she did ask me."

"Where are you going to find time to work that in?" Herc asked. "You're already juggling investigating homicides and rehabbing homes."

There couldn't have been a better time for me to announce my new plans, but now that the time had come, I found myself going shy. "I've made a decision in the last few days. Val and I want to give more back to the community that has supported us these last four years. Joining up with Project Phoenix to help low-income families find affordable housing might be one way to do that."

"I'm a hundred percent behind whatever Mom wants to do," Val said.

I took a breath and plunged ahead. "I'd like a leave of absence from the police department, Jim and Herc."

"You're quitting?" Herc asked. Luann grabbed his water glass this time.

"Not quitting, just stepping away for a while. Time enough to explore this new direction and see how compatible it is with the ethos Val and I want to pursue with Nailed It Home Renos."

"But Ro, we make such a good team."

"Time for you and Al to develop a closer relationship. And if he finds a forensic accounting position somewhere else, you also have Greg Ennis and Isla Dexter warming up in the bullpen, both anxious to join you as partner. Maybe even Janet Oliver someday, if she joins the force."

Val nudged Jim. "We'll miss you, Ro," he said. "The department has been blessed to have your expertise even on a part-time basis recently. But I get it. You've gotta do what makes sense to you."

Now Luann shoved Herc. "Yeah, I get it, too," he said. "I shoulda known something was up, the way you acted when we wrapped the case the other day."

"It's not necessarily for good, Herc. Just time to examine these new feelings."

As that discussion appeared to die down, Chuck decided to change the subject. "There's a smaller box in this big box. Why don't you show everyone what's inside?"

The next few minutes were filled with oohs and aahs as I removed my new diamond ring from its box. "How about a reenactment of my giving it to you last night?" Chuck said. He was so pleased with himself, how could I refuse?

"Okay. Just don't get too dramatic. They've just had a full meal."

He took my left hand in his. "Rowena Summerfield, I can't believe how much meeting you has changed my life. You are everything I could ever want in a lifetime partner. Will you do me the honor of becoming my wife?"

"Oh, Chuck, I never thought my life could be so rich again, but then you showed up and made me a believer. Of course, I'll marry you."

Chuck placed the ring on my finger while everyone clapped. "After she tried this on last night, she wouldn't wear it until now, so you could all be part of this momentous occasion."

Val jumped up and hugged me, then Chuck. "You two! We had no idea this was in the works." Then she turned to Chuck. "I couldn't be more pleased to welcome you to the family."

"Thanks, Val. That means a lot," Chuck told her.

"Are you going to keep your last name?" Luann asked.

"Uh …"

"We haven't gotten that far," a very wise Chuck said, sensing the topic needed further discussion.

"Or a date?" Lorna added.

One of the reasons I'd been putting Chuck off about getting married was this dread of all the attention our pending nuptials would elicit. I didn't like the spotlight aimed at me. That was what I did with others. "No. But I assure you, you'll all be the first to know as our plans move forward. And now, dessert. Who wants apple pie and who wants cherry?"

I hoped dessert would end this marriage talk. At least for now. I just needed time for it all to sink in before I started making plans.

"Thanks for not asking about our sleeping accommodations in Mount Dora," Herc said. He'd slipped into the kitchen without my noticing. It was just the two of us for now.

"That's your business, Herc. No one other than you and Luann need to know about it." And now me.

"The guy at the B&B called me early yesterday. A second room has popped up. Can you believe it? Nice Christmas present for me."

"I'm glad to hear that. It sounded like Luann was really pleased with the gift."

"Thanks to you."

He lingered even after I placed a plate of pie in each of his hands.

"Yes?" I asked.

"I'm happy for you, too, Ro. I've given Dawson a bit of trouble from time to time in the past. Guess I didn't like the idea of you having someone other than me in your life. But I'm past that. He's a good guy. Not good enough for you, of course, but I know he really cares for you."

"Thanks for saying that, Herc." My mouth had gone dry with the emotion of the moment. I couldn't say more.

He pivoted to leave and then turned back. "One more thing. It pains me to hear you say you're no longer gonna investigate cases with me. Had I not witnessed your reaction to discovering Carmen Loomis killed her boss, I'd be urging you to reconsider. But I sorta get it. They say there comes a time in everyone's life when they see a new path and must go down it. Maybe that time is coming soon for me too."

I fought to hold off the tears that were just around the corner. He wouldn't want me to go weepy on him. "You know I love you, Herc. It really helps knowing you understand."

"Yeah, well, uh, is there ice cream coming too? I love à la mode."

The scene was over.

Later that day, after everyone had left to enjoy the rest of the holiday on their own, Chuck and I sat on the couch watching the lights on the tree flicker. We'd finally taken pity on Jason, who'd been trying to paw off the Santa hat Val and Jim had stuck on him before our meal, and removed it. In return, Jason had deigned to climb onto Chuck's lap, where he promptly fell asleep. It was like he knew about our engagement and had accepted it.

"This was the best Christmas I've had in a long time, Chuck. Thank you for making me take the time to enjoy it."

"You're welcome. It was the best Christmas ever for me, and I would say that even if you hadn't accepted my ring. Though that made it more special."

"We've got quite the year ahead," I said, fingering my ring, unaccustomed to having something on that finger after so many years.

"Any regrets to saying yes?" he asked, his tone a little anxious.

I squeezed his hand. "None whatsoever. I just needed time to get to this point. You very wisely gave it to me."

"Wasn't easy. I've wanted to make what we have together permanent for some time. And Ro, if you don't want to take the name Dawson as your new last name, I'll understand."

"Can we defer that discussion until I've had more than twenty-four hours to absorb our news?"

"Of course. Let's talk about your other announcement of the day, the fact you're stepping away from investigating homicides. I'm delighted with your decision, because you know how I worry every time you accept another case. But I saw that look in your eyes the last few days. I know you're doing this for you, because it's something you have to do."

"For now." Then it occurred to me I was no longer in this alone. "Are you ready to come along for the ride?"

"More than," he said.

"Then why don't you watch a ball game while I start my plan."

SNEAK PEEK
CRAKS IN A MARRIAGE

Here's a sneak peek at *Craks in a Marriage*, Book 1 in Barbara Barrett's other cozy mystery series, The Mah Jongg Mysteries.

Olivia settled into a chair. "Before she or anyone else arrives, we need to talk." She leaned closer. "I need your help in another way. I'm a proud woman, Sydney. I don't like to rely on anyone else to solve my problems, but at the moment, I'm not in a position to do that."

Caught off guard, Sydney set down her lists, not sure what was coming. "Solve your problems? What are you talking about?" As soon as the words were out, she wanted to retract them. What was she getting herself into?

"When the sheriff pulled me into his office earlier and you waited in the outer room, it wasn't just to console me. He said there were questions about Paul he needed to ask right away."

"Questions?"

"About Paul's life. People who might bear him a grudge. People to whom he may have owed money or insulted. I told him I didn't know of anyone like that, although as a businessman in our community, he may have stepped on toes at times."

Where was she going with this? Maybe she just wanted to talk, vent. "I've never been personally involved in, uh, situations like this, but I guess that would be the kind of thing the sheriff would need to know to start his investigation."

"His *investigation*, yes. Then he started asking about Paul and me. Our marriage. Our relationship."

Uh-oh. Sydney remembered the telephone call she'd overheard. Oh, God, the sheriff wouldn't talk to Olivia's friends and acquaintances, would he? What would she tell him if he did? She wasn't one to skip over the truth. "I guess that would be part of his investigation as well."

Olivia gripped her hands in what looked like a steely prayer. "I didn't kill him, Sydney. You have to believe me."

"Okay?"

"But things haven't been what I'd describe as happy between us lately. The sheriff is sure to uncover some of that. If he does, he might stop looking for the real culprit and tie it all on me."

"But if you're innocent, how could he make the charges stick?" Sydney blurted out her question, flabbergasted at the woman's statement.

Olivia glanced away, as if not wanting to face her directly. "I can't believe I'm saying this, but I suspect Paul was being unfaithful. I was about to confront him, as soon as I had more definite proof."

Sydney opened her mouth and closed it just as fast. What could she say? What was she supposed to say?

"I know. You're surprised. To our friends and the rest of the community, even to our children, we seemed like the perfect couple. No cares in the world. So supportive of each other."

Maybe not *that* perfect, but until recently, Sydney would have agreed with the statement. "I, uh, had no idea." Okay, sometimes she did stray a *tad* from the truth. When it would hurt someone else if she was too frank.

"Paul had a straying eye. Probably part of aging. Had to prove to himself he still had the old charm. For all I know, this might not have been the first liaison. He wasn't as careful hiding things this time. That's all."

Sydney's mind skipped around, trying to connect loose ends in Olivia's words with other observations of late. Would Olivia kill Paul over an affair? Sydney couldn't dismiss the possibility, despite Olivia's claim of innocence. Olivia had admitted she was a proud woman. No doubt about that from her play at mah jongg. Would she stand by and let the man cheat on her? What if he wanted a divorce? Would she allow that to happen? Probably not. But the idea of Olivia bashing him in the head didn't wash. She might be a woman who took action, but she was precise, methodical. If she decided to off Paul, she would do it in a less sloppy way that wouldn't lead back to her.

"Did you tell that to the sheriff?

Olivia pressed her lips together. "No. Like I told you, I only suspected Paul of playing around. If he was seeing someone else, let the sheriff discover it on his own."

Sydney wondered what she'd do if she were in Olivia's place. Not that Trip would ever cheat. If for no other reason, although there were plenty of others, the man was too busy keeping himself busy in retirement to have time to mess around. "You need to prepare yourself, then. Because Sheriff Rick Formero is no pushover. If there's something to find out, he will."

"That's why I need your help."

"What? How?" This conversation was getting weirder and weirder.

"I need to spend the next few days with my children getting through the funeral and handling the estate, but I doubt the sheriff will back away from his investigation during that time. I need for you to help me discover who really did kill Paul."

Had she heard the woman correctly? "I'm not an investigator."

"That's just it. No one would suspect you of gathering information for me. But you and those cohorts of yours probably know everything that's going on in this town. Use that talent to help me clear my name."

Learn more at BarbaraBarrettBooks.com

AFTERWORD

Dear Reader,

Thank you for reading this book. If you liked it, won't you please take a minute to leave a review?

To keep up with Ro and Val's growing business and Ro's latest homicide case, sign up for my newsletter at https://www.subscribepage.com/BBCozies.

This is my second cozy mystery series. I've also written nine books in the Mah Jongg Mystery series. You can learn more about them and also the eleven contemporary romances I've published on my website, www.barbarabarrettbooks.com.

Follow me on Facebook: http://bit.ly/2aXZvG9
Follow me on X: https://twitter.com/bbarrettbooks

ACKNOWLEDGMENTS

This book would not have been possible without the input and suggestions of my editor, Chris Kridler, of Sky Diary Productions. Chris also produced the incredible cover, formatted the manuscript and put zip into the back cover blurb.

Thanks also to Sharleen Newton, Harriet Sawyer and Judie Stark for their keen proofing eyes.

As always, thanks to my husband, Veryl, for his ongoing support.

BOOKS BY BARBARA BARRETT

Cozy Mysteries

The Mah Jongg Mystery Series

Craks in a Marriage

Bamboozled

Connect the Dots

Beware the East Wind

Flower Power

Jokers Wild

The Charleston Challenge

The Dragon Lady Gets Her Due

Courtesy Call

also available in paperback

Nailed It Home Reno Mysteries

Measure Twice, Murder Once

Loose Screw

Death by Drywall

Homicide by Hammer

Nuts and Bolts

Snared by the Snake

Wrenched at the Reindeer Run

A LITTLE ABOUT
BARBARA BARRETT

Barbara Barrett started reading mysteries when she was pregnant with her first child to keep her mind off things like her changing body and food cravings. When she'd devoured as many Agatha Christies as she could find, she branched out to English village cozies and Ellery Queen.

Later, to avoid a midlife crisis, she began writing fiction at night when she wasn't at her day job in human resources for Iowa State Government. After releasing eleven full-length romance novels and two novellas, she returned to the cozy mystery genre, using one of her retirement pastimes, the game of mah jongg, as her inspiration. Not only has it been a great social outlet, it has also helped keep her mind active when not writing.

Though not an interior designer, that occupation has always fascinated Barbara. Her father was a carpenter, and her husband has his own woodworking business. Exposure to their work got her interested in watching numerous home improvement shows on HGTV. Ro and Val are an amalgam of several HGTV hosts. Barbara used that combination of personality traits for Ro and turned her into a female sleuth who rehabs older houses.

Barbara is a member of Sisters in Crime, Sinc-Iowa and Florida Star Fiction Writers.

She is married to the man she met her senior year of college. They have two grown children, eight grandchildren and two great grandchildren.

Now retired, she is a resident of Florida, although she spends her summers in Iowa, her home state, and Minnesota. She earned her B.A. degree in history from the University of Iowa and her master's degree in history from Drake University.

When not in front of her laptop creating her next story, she plays mah jongg, watches TV detective shows and enjoys lunches with friends. Most recently, she has begun to paint in acrylics and is working to evolve her skills.

www.ingramcontent.com/pod-product-compliance
Lightning Source LLC
Chambersburg PA
CBHW061240210726
48293CB00003B/845